CW00816011

The Christmas Nanny

ELIZABETH KELLY

Copyright © 2020 Elizabeth Kelly

All rights reserved.

Published by
EK Publishing Inc.

This book is the copyrighted property of the author, and may not be reproduced, scanned or distributed for commercial or non-commercial purposes. Quotes used in reviews are the exception. No alteration of content is allowed.

Your support and respect for the property of this author is appreciated.

This book is a work of fiction and any resemblance to persons, living or dead, or places, events or locales is purely coincidental. The characters are productions of the author's imagination and used fictitiously.

Cover design by
EK Designs

ISBN-13: 978-1-77446-033-7

Chapter One

Sam

"I got a solution to your problem."

I stared blankly at Mrs. Neeman. My neighbour to the left, Mrs. Neeman, was somewhere between the ages of seventy-three and ninety-nine. She walked with a cane, wore her steel-coloured hair in a bun, and didn't like to be reminded she was going deaf.

She was currently standing on my front porch wearing a bright red jacket with her feet shoved into unlaced boots. When she rang the doorbell, I'd assumed she had come over to thank me for shoveling out her driveway and sidewalk. The storm last night had blanketed the entire neighbourhood in wet, heavy snow.

"What problem is that, Mrs. Neeman?"

"Your babysitter problem," she said with an impatient sigh. "I got a solution."

"Well," I said cautiously, "Oscar is pretty high energy and I know you have arthritis. I'm not sure that you'd be able to keep up with him. I appreciate the offer though and -"

"Not me, you nitwit!" she said. "Her."

She pointed to my neighbour on the right. I stared at the tiny brunette struggling to clear her driveway of the heavy snow. A twinge of guilt went through me. If I was a good neighbour, I would have cleared her driveway too. But I hadn't really thought about it. Up until a few months ago, she'd had her own man to shovel.

"She has a job, doesn't she?" I said.

"Not anymore," Mrs. Neeman said.

"What happened?"

"For Pete's sake, Sam Black, are you going to invite me in or let me freeze to death on your damn porch?"

"Right, sorry. Come in, Mrs. Neeman," I stepped back and let the old lady clomp her way past me before shutting the door.

I hung her jacket on the hook as she took her boots off. She was wearing a canary yellow tracksuit that was more blinding than the snow outside. She followed me to the kitchen and sat down at the table with a wince.

Oscar was still finishing his breakfast and he gave Mrs. Neeman a honey-coated smile. "Hi, Mrs. Neeman."

"Hello, young man," she said.

"Do you want some toast?" He held out the last of his soggy toast. Honey dripped onto the table as Mrs. Neeman shook her head.

"Certainly not. I don't share my food and if I did, I wouldn't share it with a child. Children are germ-infested devils wrapped in adorable packaging."

"Okay," Oscar said.

Oscar didn't seem at all concerned that Mrs. Neeman considered him germ infested. Of course, he was pretty easy going for a six-year-old. I leaned down and kissed the top of his head. "Why don't you go wash up and then play in your room for a bit, bud?"

"Sure, Daddy." He slid out of his chair. Holding his sticky hands in front of him, he wandered out of the kitchen.

"Would you like a cup of tea?" I asked.

"Nope. I ain't got time for that," Mrs. Neeman said. "My Beverly will be here soon to take me to the Walgreens. I need some cream for my hemorrhoids. They've been paining me something fierce the last few days."

I was speechless for a moment. What did someone say to an old woman about her hemorrhoid pain? I settled on, "I'm sorry to hear that."

She just shrugged. "Anyway, I heard about Melody leaving you high and dry over the Christmas holidays for babysitting. I knew all along that girl would bail on you, Sam Black. I figured you could hire Tess next door to look after your boy."

"She works at the factory. Doesn't she?" I said.

"She got laid off," Mrs. Neeman said.

"How do you know that?" I asked.

"I just do," Mrs. Neeman said. "You gonna hire her or not?"

"Does she have experience with kids?"

3

"How the hell would I know?" Mrs. Neeman said. "I'm not as gossipy as that old biddy across the street."

The old biddy she was referring to was Sheila Kirkman. Sheila spent most of her days sitting at her kitchen window with a pair of binoculars in one hand and her cell phone in the other.

"Well, I appreciate the suggestion but -"

"Do you think you got the time to be picky?" Mrs. Neeman leaned forward and tapped the table with one arthritic finger. "Christmas holidays start in two days. What are you gonna do with your boy? I know you talked to Jim about getting his granddaughter to babysit and she's only sixteen. Tess is twenty-five and a lot more responsible than that awful Anna. Anna will have her boyfriend over and be busy sucking face with him instead of watching your boy. I guarantee it."

I made a face but didn't argue. Mrs. Neeman had a point about Anna and her boyfriend. Truthfully, I'd only talked to Jim because I was desperate. It hadn't mattered anyway. Anna had a part time job at Walmart and wasn't available.

"Get your ass over to Tess's house and ask her to babysit your boy. The poor girl's been struggling something awful with money since her boyfriend left her high and dry," Mrs. Neeman said.

She fixed me with a hard gaze. "You know she just rents the place from that guy who bought it after old man Wendell kicked the bucket, right?"

I nodded and Mrs. Neeman said, "Well, don't you be sayin' anything to anyone else in the neighbourhood, but I heard she's behind on her rent now that she and her boyfriend are kaput. She might be kicked out of the house at the beginning of the year. How's that for awful? Christmas is only a week and a half away for Pete's sake! How's the girl supposed to enjoy her Christmas knowing she'll be homeless after that?"

"Well, I guess it wouldn't hurt to talk to her," I said.

Mrs. Neeman rolled her eyes. "No, it wouldn't."

She heaved herself to her feet, shaking off my hand when I tried to help her. Her cane thumped on the floor as she walked to the hallway and carefully stuck her feet into her boots. I helped her into her jacket and opened the door.

"There's my Beverly," she said and walked out the door without saying goodbye.

I waved at her daughter before closing the door and heading down the hallway to Oscar's bedroom. He was sitting in his Spiderman tent and I navigated my way across the Lego-covered floor and plucked the iPad from his hands.

He grinned cheekily at me as I shut the game off and said, "You know the rules, Oscar. You already had your hour of iPad time before breakfast."

"Did I?" he said so innocently that I laughed.

"Nice try, buddy. I have to run next door for a minute to talk with Miss Walker. Can you play with your Legos while I'm gone? I'll be right outside so if you need me, just come out to the front porch. Okay?"

"Okay," Oscar said.

I ruffled his hair and picked my way back

through the minefield of Legos to the hallway. "I won't be long, buddy."

"Okay." Oscar was already reaching for the tub of Legos. I studied his face and felt a surge of love that nearly staggered me in its intensity. God, did I love this kid.

"Be right back."

"Uh-huh," Oscar didn't look up as I left his room and headed downstairs. I was just grabbing my jacket when there was a tentative knock on the door. I opened it and stared in surprise at Tess.

"Hi, Sam."

"Hey, Tess. How are you?"

"Good, thanks." Her cheeks and nose were red from the cold and she was shivering but she smiled cheerfully. She held up the broken handle of her snow shovel. "Hey, do you think I could borrow your snow shovel? I broke mine with my Hulk-like strength."

I laughed. "Actually, I was just coming out to talk to you for a minute. Why don't you come in and warm up while we chat?"

"Sure." She followed me into the house and took off her jacket and boots.

"Do you want a coffee?" I asked as we walked into the kitchen.

"I don't drink coffee." She sat down, rubbing her hands together briskly.

"Tea?"

She shook her head before rubbing her upper arms through her sweatshirt. "I'll take a hot chocolate if you have it."

"I have a six-year-old - I've got hot chocolate,"

I said. "The real question is – do you want marshmallows or not?"

"What's hot chocolate without marshmallows?" she said.

I popped the hot chocolate pod into the machine and let it do its thing as I grabbed the bag of mini marshmallows from the cupboard and set it in front of her.

"Thank you," she said when I placed the mug of chocolate next to the marshmallows.

The number of marshmallows she poured into her hot chocolate rivaled the number Oscar used. I grinned when she grabbed a handful of marshmallows from the bag and popped them directly into her mouth.

"Sorry," she said. "I may have a slight addiction to sweet stuff."

I sat down as she took a sip of hot chocolate. Tess and her boyfriend – ex-boyfriend now – had lived in the house next door for the last two years but I'd never really spoken to Tess before. I'd spoken with Roger a few times, just 'hey, how's it going' conversations while we were both working in our yards, but Tess didn't interact much with the other neighbours.

No, she didn't interact much with the male neighbours.

My inner voice had a point. Maybe Roger had been the jealous type.

I supposed if I had a woman who looked like Tess, I might be the jealous type too. She was short and slender, but her ass was nice, and her chest was on the bigger side for her frame. I wondered idly if her breasts were fake as I stared at her face. Her long and curly dark hair was currently pulled back in a ponytail, but it looked shiny and soft. Her dark brown eyes were framed with long lashes and her lips were full and kissable.

Whoa. Thinking about kissing the woman who might become my son's nanny was a very bad idea. Besides, she was in her mid-twenties and probably considered me an old man. If I hit on her, she'd, at best, think I was pathetic, and at worst, a pervert. Wasn't banging the nanny the most watched porn? I was sure I had read that somewhere.

"Sam?"

Tess stared curiously at me. I drummed my fingers on the table. "Sorry, in my own head there for a minute."

"That's okay. What did you want to talk to me about?"

"Well, I heard that you were laid off from your job."

She rolled her eyes. "Even after two years, I'm still not used to this neighbourhood's gossip network and how efficient it is."

"Sorry," I repeated.

"It's fine. It's not like I'm trying to hide it or anything." She sipped at her hot chocolate again.

"I know this is last minute and don't feel pressured to say yes, but I'm looking for a nanny for Oscar for the Christmas holidays."

She stared at me and I said, "I don't know if you even like kids but, uh, if you do, it's a steady paycheque until he goes back to school on the fourth."

"I like kids," she said.

"Okay. Don't take this the wrong way but are you good with kids? I mean, do you have experience with them?" I asked.

She smiled a little before nodding. "Yes. I did a lot of babysitting when I was younger."

"Good," I said with obvious relief in my voice. "I pay fifteen dollars an hour and I'd need you from eight to five, Monday to Friday. I'm usually home by five unless traffic in the city is bad. I'll make supper for Oscar when I get home, but you'll have to make him breakfast and lunch."

"I can do that," she said. "Quick question – what happened to Melody?"

"Did you know her?" I asked.

"Not well," she said. "But she was into running and sometimes we ended up on the same running path on the weekends."

"She and Phil broke up," I said.

"Oh. But why did she quit? She wasn't living with Phil so it's not like she was homeless and had to move out of the neighbourhood."

"She told me, and I quote," I scrunched up my face and pitched my deep voice higher into a remarkably accurate impression of my former babysitter, "I, like, totally can't ever come back here, Mr. Black. I might run into Phil and his new slut girlfriend, and I'll, like, just die."

Tess burst into laughter. I was suddenly happier than I should have been at making her laugh.

"Yeah, that sounds exactly like Melody. Sorry she bailed on you like that," she said.

I shrugged. "It's what I get for hiring a nineteen-year-old to babysit."

Tess took a sip of her hot chocolate. "Well, I'd be happy to babysit Oscar for you."

The weight fell off my shoulders, but I cautioned myself against being too relieved just yet. "I would like you to meet Oscar first. Just to make sure that he…"

I trailed off, suddenly unsure of how to word it without sounding like a total jerk.

"That he likes me?" she said.

"Yeah."

"Fair enough." She took another sip of her hot chocolate. I was inappropriately obsessed with the way she licked her bottom lip clean.

"Sam?"

"Sorry, what?" I tore my gaze away from her mouth.

"I asked if I could meet him now. I'm assuming you'll want me to start babysitting on Monday and it's already Saturday."

"Yes, of course. That's a great idea." Cursing inwardly at the way I was acting, I called for Oscar.

He tromped down the stairs, making a surprisingly loud racket for a kid who weighed less than sixty pounds, and joined us in the kitchen. "Yeah?"

"Oscar, I want you to meet Tess," I said.

"Hi, Oscar." Tess got out of the chair and squatted next to him. "I like your t-shirt."

"Thanks," Oscar said as he studied his Spiderman t-shirt. "Do you like Spiderman?"

"I do," Tess said. "But Wonder Woman is my favourite."

10

"She's cool but Spiderman is better." Oscar spied the marshmallows on the table and stared at me in excitement. "Daddy, can I have hot chocolate too?"

"Yes," I said. "Sit at the table with Tess while I make it for you."

Tess returned to her seat and Oscar sat down in the chair beside her. "You live next door to us."

"That's right."

"You have a boyfriend. He's really loud."

Tess smiled. "I used to have a boyfriend."

"What happened to him?" Oscar asked. "Did he die?"

Tess gave me a startled look. I cleared my throat and said, "Oscar, buddy, remember when we talked about how when someone goes away it doesn't mean that they died?"

"Yeah," Oscar said. "But did he die like my mommy died?"

Tess shook her head. "No. We just decided to stop dating and he moved away."

"Oh, like Daddy and Stephanie." He looked at me. "Right, Daddy?"

"Yes," I said.

"Stephanie didn't die, she just left. But my mommy died. Did you know that?" Oscar said to Tess.

"I didn't. I'm very sorry, Oscar," Tess said.

Oscar shrugged. "I didn't know her. She died before I was even born." He paused and frowned. "Wait, she died when I was born. Right, Daddy?"

I nodded as I brought him his hot chocolate. "Yes."

"Isn't that sad, Tess?" Oscar said.

I pulled the bag of marshmallows away before he could stick his hand into it. "I'll add the marshmallows, bud."

"That's very sad," Tess said.

"I have a picture of her in my room," Oscar announced. "I can show it to you if you want."

"Sure," Tess said.

"Okay, but I'm gonna drink my hot chocolate first."

He blew on his hot chocolate and then took a tiny sip around the marshmallows as I gave Tess an awkward look. Oscar rarely mentioned Stephanie now, but he was bringing up the subject of his dead mother more and more. My chest tightened. Ever since he started school and realized that the other children had mothers he'd talked about his mother more often. I suspected that he was starting to want a mother but, whether that was to fit in with his classmates or just a personal yearning, I wasn't sure.

Tess was still studying Oscar. When she reached out and smoothed down his dark hair, he said, "I like your teeth."

"Thank you," she said with a laugh.

"You mean to say you like her smile, buddy," I said.

Oscar shook his head. "Nope. I like her teeth. They're very white."

The kid had a point. Tess did have nice teeth. And a sexy bottom lip that looked very suckable.

I turned around and quickly made myself a cup of coffee. I hadn't slept with anyone since

Stephanie walked out on us two years ago. Between work and being a single dad, I didn't have time to date. Which was fine with me. I'd learned the hard way that bringing someone into Oscar's life was a mistake. He was acting like Stephanie leaving was no big deal, but my stomach was clenched into a tight ball. The memory of Oscar screaming and pleading with Stephanie not to leave was seared into my brain. I would never put him through that pain again.

So, when he's a teenager and refusing to have anything to do with you, you're just gonna what – sit alone at home?

"Do you like Legos?" Oscar asked Tess.

"I had a few Lego sets when I was a kid," Tess said.

"They had Legos when you were a kid?" Oscar gave her a suspicious look and Tess laughed.

"Bud, they had Legos when *I* was a kid," I said.

"No way, Daddy," Oscar said. "You're old."

Tess laughed again, and I actually blushed a little. "I'm not that old."

"Yes, you are." Oscar turned to Tess. "He's thirty-two. How old are you?"

"Oscar, it's not polite to ask people how old they are," I said.

"I don't mind," Tess replied. "I'm twenty-five."

"Why don't you have kids?" Oscar said. "My mommy was twenty-five when she had me. Right, Daddy?"

"Yes," I said.

"Don't you like kids?" Oscar asked.

"Oscar," I said, "you're being rude."

13

ELIZABETH KELLY

Oscar cocked his head at me. "Am I?"

"No," Tess said before I could answer. "You're just being curious. I don't have any kids because I haven't found the right person to have them with yet. But I like kids very much."

"Okay." Oscar drank some more hot chocolate before saying, "Are you dating my daddy? Is that why you're here?"

I had just taken a drink of coffee and I immediately choked on it. As I coughed and gagged and my face turned bright red, Tess hurried over to me. She thumped me firmly on the back before rubbing between my shoulders.

"You okay, Sam?"

"Good," I rasped before clearing my throat.

"You sure?"

Her hand was still rubbing my back and holy shit, did it feel good. Too good. I was about to get an erection from just the touch of her hand. I pulled away from her immediately. I set my coffee cup on the counter as embarrassment crossed her face.

"Sorry," she said.

"No," I shook my head, "it's fine. I just…"

What exactly was I about to say? Sorry, I was so rude but your hand on my back was about to give me a stiffy and I didn't want my six-year-old to see it? If that didn't scream *pervert*, what did?

Tess had returned to her seat and Oscar smiled at her. "Are you dating my daddy?"

Well, shit. I was hoping my choking had distracted him.

"No," Tess said. "I'm not dating your daddy."

"Oh. Then why are you here?"

"Oscar," I sat down beside him, "Tess is going to be your nanny during the Christmas break. She'll come over every day while I'm at work."

"Where's Melody?" Oscar asked.

"She can't babysit you this time," I replied. "So, Tess is going to do it instead."

"Okay," Oscar said with a shrug. "Will you play with me? Melody was on her phone a lot."

Guilt trickled into my gut. Why didn't Oscar tell me that?

"I'll play with you, little man," Tess said. "I promise."

"Okay," Oscar said. "You wanna see my Legos?"

"Sure," Tess said. "If it's okay with your dad."

"Yes," I said.

"C'mon, Tess!" Oscar slid off the chair, grabbed her hand and pulled on it. Tess stood and gave me a sweet smile that made my dick twitch in my pants. As Oscar tugged her out of the kitchen and down the hall, I turned and stared blankly out the kitchen window. Oscar seemed to really like Tess and my babysitter issue was solved. I should have been happy. So, why was I feeling so uneasy?

Maybe because you want to bang the nanny?

I groaned and grabbed my coffee, dumping the rest of it down the sink. I was not inappropriately lusting after my son's temporary nanny. That was just asking for trouble.

Chapter Two

Tess

"You're late, Tess."

"I know, I'm sorry." I squeezed past the trio of shoppers standing in line for coffee and sank into the chair beside my best friend, holding onto the snow shovel with one hand. "Is that for me?"

She nodded and handed me the cup. "Hot chocolate with extra whip, extra chocolate sprinkles, and a splash of diabetes."

I made a face at her before taking a sip. "Thank you, Penny."

"You're welcome. Why are you carrying a snow shovel?"

"Mine broke yesterday morning when I was trying to shovel the driveway," I said.

"You should have texted me. I would have sent Bill over," Penny said.

"That's sweet but you live half an hour away and with the snow, it would have been more like an hour," I said.

Penny's phone buzzed, and she held up her hand. "Hold on. I gotta answer this text."

I stared at the shovel in my hand and took another sip of hot chocolate. The Starbucks was filled to the brim with holiday shoppers and I pulled the shovel a little closer to me when a larger man tried to slide by our table.

"One more minute, babe," Penny said.

I made a 'no problem' gesture with my hand. Penny was in her late thirties and I knew some of the other employees at the factory had found our friendship a little odd, but I'd always hung out with people older than me. Before my mom died, she'd told me on more than one occasion that I had an old soul.

She wasn't wrong. I'd always felt older than my age, and I wasn't naïve or stupid enough to realize that was part of the reason that Roger had left me. At twenty-six, he was still stuck firmly in party mode. My refusal to join him in partying every weekend and my lack of interest in drinking and in smoking weed, had at first confused him, then pissed him off. We'd tried to make it work for two years but could an introvert and an extrovert ever really be happy together? Our differences in how we wanted to spend our free time had eventually driven a wedge between us that couldn't be fixed.

Was that all it was? Or was it also his low IQ and his lackluster abilities in the bedroom?

I immediately scolded myself. It wasn't Roger's fault that he preferred playing video games and smoking weed over having a conversation. Not everyone was a scholar. The bad sex on the other hand…

I sighed and took another sip of hot chocolate. I didn't have a lot of experience, but I knew a poor performance in the bedroom when I saw one. Or was it felt one? Either way, Roger's foreplay technique of a minute of kissing, a squeeze or two to the boobs, and then straight to the sex wasn't exactly enough to get me in the mood.

Don't forget about his weirdly small and crooked penis.

"Okay, done. Sorry… Bill is out Christmas shopping and he couldn't remember if his mother wanted the twelve-cup muffin tin or the twenty-four." Penny rolled her eyes. "Who asks for a muffin tin for Christmas? What were you just thinking about? You looked all moody and dramatic."

"Roger," I said.

"Why the hell would you be thinking about old tiny bent dick?"

"Penny, shh!" I scolded.

Penny just shrugged. "What? If you didn't want me talking about his bent little penis, you shouldn't have told me about it."

I tried not to laugh and failed miserably. Penny was loud and occasionally rude, but she was also kind and generous. I adored her.

"I don't know why I was thinking about him," I said. "I haven't heard a word from him since he left."

"Do you miss him?" Penny asked. "I mean, I know you're not missing his failed attempts to make you climax but -"

"Penny!"

"*But* are you missing having him around to do the household blue jobs?" She eyed the shovel in my hand.

"No," I said. "Besides, my neighbour finished shoveling my driveway for me."

"Which neighbour?" Penny demanded. "Hot single dad neighbour, or balding probably masturbates to pictures of the Queen neighbour?"

I laughed again. "Ralph doesn't masturbate to pictures of the Queen, Penny."

"You can't possibly know that for sure." Penny sipped at her coffee. "So, who was it?"

"Sam," I said.

"Ooh, lovely. Was he shirtless? Wearing a kilt? Did you know that you can hire men in kilts to come shovel your driveway?"

"No, he wasn't shirtless or wearing a kilt," I said. "Why would he wear a kilt?"

"He looks like a man who'd wear a kilt," Penny said. "He's got the legs for it. Remember last summer when he was doing that strip tease in his yard?"

"He was not doing a strip tease in his yard," I said. "He took his shirt off while he was mowing the lawn."

"Best fifteen minutes of my life," Penny said. "He's a single dad, shouldn't he have a dad bod? I mean what friggin' dad do you know that has a six pack like that?" She gave me a dreamy look. "I rode Bill like a damn pony that night. Between you and me, I might have been thinking about those spectacular abs on your neighbour the whole time."

I laughed again. "He has a good body but so did Roger."

"True," Penny said. "But Roger was built like a brick shithouse and I like my men all lean and trim like your single dad. The thick neck and the biceps the size of my head just don't do it for me. Hey, you ever think that maybe Roger did steroids? It would explain the tiny penis, right?"

"I don't know, and I don't care. Roger and I are over."

"Good point. So, how did you repay your sexy neighbour for the snow shoveling? Did you invite him in and give him a quick handie in the hallway? Or did you really pull out all the stops and blow him? That snow was heavy as shit, totally worth a blow job."

"Oh my God, Penny," I said. "Seriously? I love you but if you don't stop talking about hand jobs and blow jobs, I'm leaving."

"All right, all right. Don't get your good girl panties in a bunch," Penny said. "So, the neighbour shovelled your driveway and you baked him a tray of cookies to say thanks. Right?"

"No cookies. But I did accept his job offer to babysit his son during the Christmas holiday."

"Are you shitting me?" Penny said. "You're going to babysit his little rugrat?"

I nodded. "Yes. It beats working at a retail store which is about all that's available right now. And even that's just seasonal."

Penny reached across the table and squeezed my hand. "I'm sorry you got laid off at the factory, babe. If I had known it was coming down the pipes, I would have warned you."

"It's okay. Shit happens, right?"

"You gonna look for another factory job?"

"No. The day I was laid off, I applied for the animal technician program at the college. I found out yesterday that I was accepted."

Penny grinned at me. "Good for you, babe. I know you've been wanting to do that."

"I have," I said. "The only thing stopping me was Roger and his allergy to cats. Now that I don't have to worry about killing him because I have cat hair on my clothes, I can actually work as an animal technician at a vet's office. Oh, and I picked up all the supplies I need for my cat. I'm going to the humane society tomorrow night to pick out my new kitten."

"You know if you become one of those chicks who only posts pictures of their cats on their Facebook, I'm gonna disown you, right?"

"I'll keep the cat pictures to a minimum."

"Good. When do you start at the college?" Penny asked.

"The program starts in May. I'll need to find a part time job while I'm in school. I have enough savings to cover my expenses, but I'd prefer to only dip into those if I have no other option. The money I make for babysitting Oscar will pay my rent for December. In the new year, I'll apply with a temp agency, so I can avoid eating into my savings as much as possible."

"It's a fine plan," Penny said. "I'm proud of you, babe."

"Thanks, Penny." I took another drink of my hot chocolate.

"So, you gonna bang hot single dad, or what?"

"You did hear me just say that he's my new employer, right?"

"Yep. But you're hot, he's hot, and every man has a 'bang the nanny' fantasy. Guarantee you he's already thought about it," Penny said.

"No, he hasn't," I replied. "Sam isn't interested in me. I've been single for a while now and he hasn't even said a word to me, let alone hit on me. I'm not his type."

"How do you know?" Penny said.

"Just a feeling. I did find out that his wife died in childbirth. How sad is that?"

"Very sad," Penny said.

"It is." I traced the worn wood of the table with my finger.

"I'm surprised you didn't already know," Penny said. "Didn't you say that everyone knows everyone else's business in your neighbourhood?"

"Yeah," I said, "but I try to ignore most of the gossip that gets passed around. I'm probably the only one in the neighbourhood who didn't know."

"Well, I'm very glad you got at least a temporary job, and keep in mind my suggestion that you bang him," Penny said, "but I gotta go in, like, five minutes, so let's talk about Christmas. You'll be off Christmas Day and Boxing Day, right? There's still time for me to book your ticket. It's not that long of a flight so you could fly in Christmas Eve and fly back home late on Boxing Day. I already talked to Bill and he said it was fine

22

with him. We can pay for half of it as our Christmas present to you."

I shook my head. "Nope, I'm not intruding on Christmas at Bill's family cabin in Montana. One, I don't even know Bill's family, and two, I have a job now. Two days isn't long enough to brave the madness of the air travel at Christmas."

"I really hate the idea of you being all alone at Christmas," Penny said.

"I'll be okay," I said.

"Will you?"

"Yes. It's not like it's my first Christmas without my mom," I said.

"I know, but it is your first Christmas being alone," she said. "You had Bill and me that first year and Roger the next two years."

"I'll be fine," I said again. "I'm going to make nachos and watch all my favourite movies and not get out of my pajamas once. I'm looking forward to it. I swear."

Penny stared suspiciously at me. I widened my smile. I wasn't exactly lying to Penny. I would be fine at Christmas but I sure as hell wasn't looking forward to it. Still, I refused to muscle in on Penny's vacation. I would get through the holidays just fine on my own.

❧ ❦

It snowed the entire time I ran my errands and had coffee with Penny. By the time I headed for home, the roads were slick and crowded with people doing their Christmas shopping. The drive home was stressful, but as I pulled onto my street, I immediately felt calm wash over me. I loved this neighbourhood. I loved the big, old trees that lined the street and the way each home was unique. The thought of living in one of the newer housing developments with their identical houses and slivers of space between each house made me shudder.

I couldn't stop the smile when I pulled up to my house. I parked on the street instead of my driveway and watched for a few minutes as Sam and Oscar shoveled my driveway. Well, Oscar tried. He was adorable trailing after his dad with his tiny plastic shovel.

His dad's pretty damn adorable too.

Yep, he was. I'd be lying if I said that Penny was the only one who thought of Sam and his abs during sex. I'm not proud of it, but there was more than one time where the only way I could get off while Roger was on top of me was by closing my eyes and picturing Sam. It made me a terrible girlfriend. It was probably good that Roger had finally dumped me. What woman thought about her neighbour while she was having sex with her boyfriend?

Plenty, if they look like Sam.

My inner voice had a point. Sam was a damn good-looking man. There was something about his tall, lean body that set my nerve endings on fire every time I looked at him. Maybe it was the way he always looked so confident and sure of himself. His short dark hair and blue eyes only added to the appeal. And the way his face softened whenever he looked at his son? It made me want to crawl into his bed and tell him my ovaries were open for business.

Uh, Tess? You think maybe you could rein in your crush on your new boss? Also, keep in mind that the man has no interest in you. He couldn't get away from you fast enough when you touched him yesterday. What was with the rubbing, by the way?

I could feel my cheeks heating. I couldn't resist rubbing his back. He was wearing a long-sleeved thermal shirt, but I was picturing the way he looked when he did yard work without his shirt. The muscles in his back flexing and twisting as he cleared out the small flower beds that lined the front of his house. The little beads of sweat that dripped down his abdominal muscles. What I wouldn't give to trace those muscles with my tongue. To unbutton his pants and –

Tess! Knock it off, idiot!

Yep, I needed to stop that train of thought immediately. Touching him the way I did yesterday was stupid and I needed to do a better job of keeping my hands to myself. I shut off the car and climbed out, grabbing my new shovel from the trunk before heading up the driveway.

"Hi, Tess!" Oscar waved excitedly as I joined them.

"Hi, Oscar."

"I'm helping Daddy shovel!"

"You're doing a great job, little man," I said.

"I know," Oscar replied.

I laughed and Sam grinned at me. Good gravy, that dimple was a distraction I didn't need.

"Hi, Tess."

"Hi, Sam. You didn't have to shovel again. I

was just out buying a new one." I showed him the shovel.

"I don't mind," he said. "It's good exercise for us. Isn't it, Oscar?"

"Yep," Oscar said.

"Well, I really appreciate it." I stuck my shovel into the snow and cleared a path to the edge of the driveway.

"You don't have to do that," Sam said.

I laughed. "It's my driveway so I should at least pitch in for the last half of it. Besides, it's good exercise for me too."

Sam just nodded before turning away and continuing to shovel. I groaned inwardly. My attempts at flirting were ridiculous. Also – I really needed to stop even trying to flirt.

New boss, Tess. Flirting equals bad. Very bad.

I dug my shovel into the snow and tried to pretend like I wasn't attracted to my insanely hot neighbour.

It took us less than ten minutes to finish clearing the driveway. Oscar had gotten bored and wandered away to dig a hole in the snow covering my yard. As Sam knocked the snow off his shovel, he said, "Oscar, time to go inside."

"I'm digging, Daddy!"

"It's lunch time, buddy."

Oscar tromped over to join us. He took Sam's hand, and my ovaries cried out for mercy when Sam gave him a smile that radiated love.

"Why don't you come in and I'll make you lunch," I blurted out.

Sam blinked at me. "What?"

Tess! What are you doing?

"Lunch," I said. "I'll make you and Oscar lunch to say thank you for shoveling my driveway."

Oscar cocked his head at me. "Do you know how to make grilled cheese sandwiches?"

I squatted and smiled at him. "Secretly, I make the best grilled cheese sandwiches in the world."

"Nu-uh, Daddy does."

"Are you sure?"

"Yes," Oscar said.

I laughed and booped the tip of his cold nose. "I still think you should join me for lunch, and I'll make you grilled cheese sandwiches."

Oscar stared up at Sam. "Can we, Daddy? Please?"

Sam hesitated. I stood and resisted the sudden urge to boop his nose. Holy crap, my flirting skills were getting worse by the minute.

"Join me," I said. "I'd really like to say thank you."

Sam glanced across the street at Sheila Kirkman's house. Instantly, I knew what the issue was. I shrugged and said, "You and I both know that we're already the gossip of the neighbourhood. The minute I went into your house yesterday, it started."

"True," Sam said. He rolled his eyes before squeezing Oscar's hand. "Let's go in and try Tess's grilled cheese, buddy."

Chapter Three

Sam

"Well, what do you think?" Tess wiggled her eyebrows at Oscar as he chewed the bite of sandwich.

"It's good," he said. "I like Daddy's better."

Tess clapped her hand over her heart and said, "You cut me deep, Oscar."

I laughed as Oscar gave her a puzzled look before taking another bite. "It's good."

"Eat some of the veggies, please," I said.

Oscar wrinkled his nose before selecting the smallest carrot from the plate of raw veggies Tess had placed on the table. Tess slid my sandwich onto a plate and set the plate in front of me.

"Thank you," I said.

"You're welcome." She turned away and my gaze dropped to her ass. Her jeans were tight, her ass was firm, and I was a pervert. I looked away and took a bite of my sandwich. It was good, better than mine, and I immediately told her that.

She laughed as she flipped her sandwich in the pan. "You're just trying to make me feel better."

"I'm not," I said. "Oscar has weird taste."

"No, I don't," Oscar said. He had already finished one half of his sandwich and was starting on the second half.

"Veggies, Oscar," I prompted before picking up a slice of cucumber and popping it into my mouth.

He ate the carrot as he stared at Tess's kitchen. "Your cupboard is broken." He pointed at the tall pantry. The door was propped up against the wall next to it and Oscar studied the boxes and cans of food lined up neatly on the shelves. "Why did it break?"

"I don't know," Tess said as she sat down beside him. "I just opened the door last week and it fell off in my hand."

"Must be your Hulk-like strength," I teased, then immediately cursed myself for flirting with her.

She laughed. "Must have been."

"I could probably fix it for you. I'm handy with stuff like that."

"Well, that would be really nice of you but don't feel like you have to," she said. "I can ask Bill to fix it."

"Who's Bill?" Oscar asked. For once I was happy that my kid had no filter. "Is he your boyfriend?"

"No," Tess said. "He's my friend's husband."

"Oh." Oscar finished his sandwich and ate another carrot.

"I really don't mind," I said. "Probably the

screws just came out from the hinges – sometimes they can loosen. It's an easy fix."

"Thanks, Sam. That's really nice of you." She gave me a sweet smile and damn if my dick didn't twitch again.

"I have to pee," Oscar said.

"The bathroom is right down the hallway," Tess said. "Do you want me to show you where?"

"Nope, I can find it." Oscar slid off his chair.

"Don't forget to wash your hands," I said as he left the kitchen.

"I know, Daddy," he said.

Tess grinned at the irritation in his voice. "He's adorable."

"Thanks, I think I'll keep him. The first few years were a little touch and go, but he's growing on me."

She laughed again. "Fair enough. It must be tough being a single dad."

"My mom lived close by for the first few years and she helped out a lot."

"That's nice." Tess ate more of her sandwich and I tried not to stare at her mouth.

"It was," I said. "She and my dad moved to Arizona when Oscar was three. She didn't want to, but she has bad arthritis and the cold weather was really tough on her. We fly out there a couple times a year and she spends about a month every summer with us. We Facetime a lot too."

"That's good. It's important to have family around," Tess said. "What about, uh, your wife's family?"

"Susan was an only child. Her dad died when

she was twenty. Her mom had some issues with drugs and alcohol, and Susan had cut ties with her before I even met her."

Tess made a low sound of sympathy. I said, "What about your family?"

"Only child raised by a single mom," Tess said.

"You must be close to her."

"I was," Tess replied. "She died three years ago."

"I'm sorry," I said.

"Me too. I miss her a lot. She was getting a lot of headaches. They did some scans and found a tumour in her brain. It was malignant with no real options for treatment. The doctors gave her six months to live and told her to make a bucket list."

"Jesus, that's rough," I said.

She nodded. "It was. But we made her bucket list and we almost completed the whole thing before she died. So, there's that, right?"

"Yes," I said.

"Anyway," Tess cleared her throat and quickly wiped at her face, "my dad never wanted anything to do with me, so I don't have a relationship with him. My mom has a sister in Wyoming, but I'm not close with her."

"Hey, Tess?" Oscar had returned, and he held up the blue litter scoop he was carrying in one chubby hand. "Why you got a little shovel with holes in it? It can't pick up anything."

"It's a litter scoop for cats," Tess said. "When they go to the bathroom in the litter box, you scoop it out with that."

"You have a cat?" Oscar said excitedly. "Can I

31

see it?"

"I don't have a cat yet," Tess said. "I'm going tomorrow night to pick out a kitten at the humane society."

"Oh." Oscar's excitement faded. "Daddy, can we go home now? I want to watch *Frozen*."

"Sure. Can you say thank you to Tess for making you lunch?"

"Thank you, Tess, for making me lunch," Oscar parroted.

"You're welcome, Oscar. I'll see you tomorrow, okay?"

"Sure."

"Can I help you clean up before we go?" I asked.

Tess shook her head. "No, it won't take me long."

We walked to the front door and I helped Oscar into his jacket before reaching for my own. As he put his boots on, I smiled at Tess. "Okay, well, I'll see you tomorrow morning at eight then?"

"On the dot," she said. "Thanks again for shoveling the driveway."

"You're welcome." I shoved my feet into my boots and then stood awkwardly in the hallway. I knew I needed to leave but there was an absurd part of me that wanted to invite Tess over to watch *Frozen* with us.

"Daddy, let's go!" Oscar tugged at my jacket.

"Okay, bye, Tess."

"Bye, Sam. Bye, Oscar."

"Bye," Oscar said. He opened the front door and I followed him out into the cold.

ॐ ॐ

Tess

"Hey, Tess?"

"Yeah?"

"I like you better than Melody."

I laughed and patted Oscar on his back as he knelt on the kitchen chair. "You're just saying that because I let you lick the icing from the bowl."

"No, I'm not," Oscar said earnestly. "Melody never made cookies with me. She just played on her phone all day."

I took the tray of cookies out of the oven and set them on the stove top to cool before returning to the table. "Well, I promise to try and not be on my phone too much when we're together. Okay?"

"Okay. You're doing a pretty good job," Oscar said. "I made cookies with Stephanie once, but they got really black in the oven and she got mad and started crying."

I was intensely curious about Stephanie. While part of me was ashamed I was about to interrogate a six year old for information on his dad's ex-girlfriend, I couldn't help myself.

"Stephanie was Daddy's girlfriend?"

"Uh-huh." Oscar stuck his tongue out in concentration as he smeared icing on the cookie. "She was really pretty. Prettier than you."

Ouch. That's what I got for snooping.

He glanced up at me, icing dripping from the piping tip. "You have nicer teeth though."

"Thanks," I said. "How old were you when

Daddy started dating Stephanie?"

"I dunno," he said. "I was four when she left to sing. She said she would video call me every night, but she didn't. I only talked to her a couple of times and then she didn't call anymore, and she never answered the phone when I called her. Daddy said she was busy singing. Do you like to sing, Tess?"

"Sometimes," I said.

Oscar dragged the piping tip across the cookie, leaving another wavy smeared line of icing behind. "I wanted Daddy and me to go with Stephanie and sing too, but Daddy said no. He said he couldn't leave his job."

He glanced up at me. "But one night, when Daddy didn't know I was playing in the closet, I heard him and Stephanie talking in their room. Daddy said we could move with her so she could sing and still be with us, but she said no. She said she couldn't sing and be a mom to me. She said I was too much work. Then Daddy got mad at her and she yelled at him and made him sleep on the couch."

"What she said isn't true, little man," I said. "She shouldn't have said that. Did you tell Daddy you heard them talking?"

He shrugged. "No. Daddy was really sad after Stephanie left. I was sad too. I cried a lot. He let me eat mac and cheese and play video games on his iPad for a long time. And one time we watched cartoons all day and ate an entire bucket of ice cream."

I stroked his dark hair. "You're not too much work, Oscar. Okay? You're an awesome kid and I like spending time with you."

"When we're done making cookies, can I watch *Frozen* again?" he said.

"How about we play in your room instead," I said. "Your dad said only two hours of TV time a day, remember?"

"Can I wear my *Frozen* dress while we play?" Oscar asked.

I nodded. I'll admit I was a little surprised when Oscar had dragged the Elsa Halloween outfit from his closet before we watched *Frozen* this morning. He explained that he always wore his Elsa costume when he watched the movie.

"Daddy doesn't mind?" I helped him tug the dress over his Spiderman t-shirt and jeans.

Oscar gave me a strange look. "Why would Daddy mind?"

"He wouldn't," I said. "That was a silly question."

My admiration for Sam had immediately gone up about a billion points. Roger had been nowhere near ready to have kids, but even if he were, he would never have let our son play dress-up with an Elsa costume.

"Oops," Oscar said. "I messed this one up too, Tess."

I studied the blob of icing in the middle of the Christmas tree shaped sugar cookie.

"I'm sorry." Oscar looked close to tears and I put my arm around him and gave him a quick squeeze.

"It's fine, little man. The cookies don't have to be perfect. That looks like an ornament."

"Yeah?" Oscar said.

"Yes," I replied. "Finish icing that cookie and I'll make some hot chocolate. We can drink it while we wait for those other cookies to cool. Okay?"

"Okay." Oscar bent over his cookie and I couldn't resist stroking his soft dark hair. He was a cute kid and while I was sure he had his moments like all kids did, he was pretty easy to babysit.

"Are you gonna make the hot chocolate?" Oscar raised his eyebrows at me, and I laughed at how much he looked like Sam.

"Yes, I'll do that right now." I pressed a kiss on the top of his head before moving to the counter.

ૐ ૐ

Sam

I was greeted by the smell of cookies when I opened the front door. I set my work bag on the floor and hung up my jacket before taking off my boots. I checked the kitchen first, grinning a little at the tray of sugar cookies sitting on a plate on the table. They were tree-shaped and covered in blobs and squiggles of icing that could have only come from Oscar's hand.

I grabbed a cookie and bit into it as I stuck my head into the living room. The cookie was delicious, although maybe a little too sweet for me with the icing. The living room was empty, and I walked upstairs to Oscar's room. His room was at the far end of the hallway, and I could hear Tess's soft laughter as I approached.

I leaned against the door jamb and watched the two of them. They were sitting cross-legged on the floor with their knees touching. Oscar was wearing his Elsa dress, but he had put the crown on Tess. I blinked in surprise. Oscar was fiercely possessive of his Elsa dress and crown.

"Now make this face!" Oscar said.

He pulled his nose up until it resembled a pig's snout and then stuck his tongue out at Tess. She did the same, and it was a little disconcerting to realize that I still found her sexy as hell. I rapped my knuckles on the door jamb and Tess made the cutest squeak of surprise.

"Hi, Daddy. We're making faces," Oscar said.

"I see that," I said.

Tess blushed and scrambled to her feet, swiping a hand self-consciously across her butt before smiling at me. "Hi, Sam."

"Hi, Tess. How did it go today?"

"Good, I think."

Oscar ran over and wrapped his arms around my legs. "We watched *Frozen* in the morning and then we played Twister and Connect Four, and I beat Tess at Connect Four, Daddy."

"Wow, that's pretty good," I said.

"Yep. Then we made cookies after lunch. Tess said I did a good job at decorating them."

"You did," I said. "I've already eaten one."

Oscar laughed, and I leaned down to give him a kiss. "Sounds like you had fun with Tess."

"I did," he said. "Can Tess stay for dinner?"

"Oh, um…" Oscar had never once asked if Melody could stay for dinner.

"I can't," Tess said. "I'm going to the humane society to pick out a kitten, remember?"

Oscar's eyes widened. "I want to go with you!" He ran back to her and grabbed her hand, squeezing it and giving her a pleading look. "Please, Tess! I wanna see the kittens too."

Tess smiled at him. "It's okay with me if it's okay with your dad."

"Please, Daddy!" Oscar's voice was headed into whining territory. I tried to tell myself it was to stop the whining and not my own desire to spend time with Tess that made me agree so quickly.

"Sure. If you're positive you don't mind?" I said.

"Not at all," Tess replied. "I'm leaving around six thirty. Does that give you enough time for dinner?"

"Why don't the three of us go out for dinner before we go to the humane society," I said. "My treat."

Oscar clapped his hands excitedly. "Taco Bell! I wanna go to Taco Bell!"

Before I could tell him to pick something a little healthier, Tess grinned at him. "Taco Bell is my favourite, Oscar."

"Mine too!" Oscar shouted.

"Taco Bell it is, then," I said.

Oscar jumped up and down before raising his fist triumphantly. "Tonight, we dine at...Taco Bell!"

Tess and I broke out into simultaneous laughter as Oscar gave us a huge grin. "I'm funny, Daddy."

"You are, bud," I said. "Are you wearing your

Elsa costume to the humane society?"

"Nah. I don't want to get cat stuff on it. Help me take it off, Tess." Oscar turned to Tess and raised his arms. She tugged the dress over his head and draped it across his bed before taking off the crown and setting it next to the dress.

"Okay, I'm ready," Oscar said.

"I need to go home first," Tess said. "Can I meet you outside in ten minutes?"

"Sure. That'll give me time to change," I said.

She studied my suit before smiling at me. "Maybe a little too fancy for Taco Bell."

"Yep, and," Oscar was leaning against my legs again and I reached down and tickled him until he burst into giggles, "I don't want to get cat stuff on it."

Chapter Four

Tess

I watched the black and white cat wind its way around Sam's lower legs. He reached down and stroked its back. It arched and purred and rubbed against him again. As I watched his long fingers rub the side of the cat's face, I decided it was much too weird that I wished I was the damn cat.

I concentrated on the little orange tabby I was holding. Her name was Marmalade, she was fourteen months old, and I was already completely smitten with her. We had walked into the cat room at the humane society and I thought Oscar was going to lose his mind with excitement. Cats of all colours and ages were wandering freely around the room. Some were sitting or sleeping in the big overstuffed and clawed up armchairs, some perched on top of the multiple scratching posts scattered around the room, and others had curled up in the empty cardboard boxes or cat beds that were placed in various spots in the room.

Three volunteers were in the room and I wasn't at all surprised when one of them made an immediate beeline for Sam. She had latched onto him with the fierceness of a winter storm, but I couldn't blame her. He was damn hot. It was a bit unsettling that jealousy brewed to life in my stomach when she touched his arm and giggled and flirted. I was mollified by the fact that Sam seemed completely immune to her flirting. Either he totally didn't catch on to her flirting, or he wasn't into blonde women with amazing curves.

He knew she was flirting with him. Maybe he just prefers dark-haired women with slender bodies.

Yeah, maybe. I turned my attention back to Marmalade when she butted my chin with her forehead. She purred loudly as I scratched her throat.

"She's cute."

Sam was suddenly standing next to me and I had to stop myself from leaning into his body. God, he smelled good. I don't know what aftershave he used but it smelled delicious. I shifted Marmalade in my arms and tried to ignore the way my girlie parts were starting to tingle.

"I like her," I said.

"So, she's the one?" he asked.

"She's the one."

"That's great."

He reached out to pet Marmalade just as I did, and our fingers brushed. He immediately jerked his hand away and I tried not to let my disappointment show. It was only a brief touch, but butterflies had swarmed to life in my stomach and I was suddenly much too warm.

"Sorry," I said.

"My fault," he said before searching the room for Oscar. "Oscar? Buddy, it's time to go."

"Daddy! I found a kitten for Tess," Oscar said from behind us.

We turned, and my jaw dropped as Sam made a croaking sound of surprise. Oscar was holding a large grey, long-haired cat around the middle of its body. Its front paws draped over Oscar's shoulders and its fluffy tail dragged along the ground as Oscar smiled happily at us. Despite the awkward way Oscar was holding it, the cat lounged contently against him.

"Is that cat missing a leg?" Sam said.

"Yep," I said, "and an eye."

"What the…"

Sam trailed off as the cat turned its head to stare at us. The sunken socket where his left eye used to be was more than a little disturbing. His muzzle was covered in pale scars and a big chunk was missing from his nose. His right eye, a bright green orb of colour, studied us for a moment before judging us lacking. He turned his gaze to Oscar and the little boy giggled when the cat licked his chin with his scratchy tongue.

"He likes me, Daddy!"

"Oscar, buddy, Tess has already -"

"Do you like him, Tess?" Oscar asked eagerly. "The lady said his name is One-Eyed Jack and he's been here a really long time."

"I can't imagine why," Sam muttered into my ear.

I tried not to laugh as one of the volunteers approached us and said, "How are we doing? Need any help?"

"We want this one!" Oscar said.

"Buddy, no," Sam said. "Tess has already picked out her kitten."

Oscar studied the orange cat in my arms. "But I like One Eyed Jack."

"It's Tess who's getting the cat, remember?" Sam said.

Oscar's face drew down into a pout and he held the big grey cat a little tighter. "But Jack likes me."

"I know he looks a bit rough," the volunteer said, "but Jack is actually a great cat. He's very laid back and he likes other cats, so he and Marmalade would get along just fine."

"My landlord is only allowing me to have one cat," I said.

I stared at Oscar's sweet face, torn between my desire to have Marmalade and my desire not to hurt Oscar's feelings.

"Tess," Oscar said, "why don't you like Jack?"

"It isn't that she doesn't like him," Sam said. "It's just that she also likes Marmalade. Marmalade will be a better cat for Tess than Jack. Besides, Jack will find a new home, won't he?"

He gave the volunteer a pointed look. She nodded. "He sure will. In fact, if no one takes him home tonight, tomorrow he's going to a beautiful farm."

"He is?" Oscar said.

"Yes," the volunteer said. "There are lots of other cats to play with and fields of catnip for him to roll in. He'll be very happy."

Oh God, I was getting a bad feeling in the pit of my stomach. I stared at Sam. He looked as alarmed as I felt.

As Oscar buried his face in Jack's fur, Sam said to the volunteer, "Are you saying what I think you're saying?"

The volunteer nodded. "We have a lot of cats right now and not enough room. Jack's old and most people are grossed out by the missing leg, eye, and scars."

"So, tomorrow One-Eyed Jack's going to be…" I couldn't say it.

"One-Eyed Jack will be walking with Jesus tomorrow," the volunteer said in a cheerful voice. "Now, let me get the paperwork started for Marmalade."

As she walked away, I stared wide-eyed at Sam. "Sam…"

He studied Oscar and the old grey cat before staring at me. "Well, shit."

❧ ❧

Sam

"You did a good thing, Sam."

"That's easy for you to say. *Your* cat has all her limbs and eyes. *Mine* looks like he's been through a meat grinder," I replied.

Tess laughed, and I sighed as One-Eyed Jack stood up from Oscar's pillow and meandered down to the end of the bed. He was surprisingly nimble for only having three legs. After returning from the humane society, Tess had taken Marmalade to her place and gotten her settled in before returning to our house. She'd brought a cardboard box filled with litter and a baggie of food. When Oscar insisted she stay and play with him and One-Eyed Jack, she hadn't argued. Just sat in the living room with him as Oscar dragged a piece of string for the cat to chase.

"Oscar loves him," Tess said.

"True," I said, "and it was a lot easier getting him into bed when there was a cat to go with him. Thanks for reading him a bedtime story, by the way."

"You're welcome. I was surprised by how quickly he fell asleep," Tess said. "If you have an extra car seat, I could take Oscar shopping tomorrow for some supplies for Jack."

"That would be great," I said. "It'll save me stopping after work."

The cat sat down on the end of the bed, lifted his remaining back leg, and licked his own ass.

"That Jack, such a charmer," I said.

Tess laughed again. I stared down at her as she stood in the doorway of Oscar's bedroom. She was beautiful, and I had the strongest urge to lean down and kiss her. I desperately wanted to know what her lips tasted like.

"Sam?" Tess said in a low voice. "What's wrong?"

"Nothing," I said as I took a step back. "Why?"

"You looked weird for a minute there," she said.

"I'm fine. But it's getting late so…"

"Right," she said as her cheeks reddened.

"Sorry, I didn't mean to overstay my welcome."

"No, you didn't," I said. "Really. I just know that you probably want to spend some time with Marmalade, and you've had to spend most of your day with Oscar, so…"

She gave me a small smile. "I don't mind. I like Oscar."

"He likes you too," I said as I studied her mouth. "A lot."

There was a moment of awkward silence and then Tess smiled again at me. "Okay, well, I'd better go then."

"Right," I said. My idea of inviting her to stay for a nightcap and then giving her a tour of my bedroom - in particular, my bed - was a terrible idea.

I followed her down the hallway, leaning against the wall as she shrugged into her jacket and pulled on her boots. "Okay, well, bye."

"Bye, Tess."

She hesitated, and I clenched my hands into fists behind my back. If she didn't leave soon, I'd say to hell with being proper and find out just how sweet her lips tasted.

"Okay, bye," she repeated before opening the door and slipping out into the cold. I stood on the porch and waited until she was safely in her own house before returning to mine. I closed the door, locked it, and leaned against it. I really needed to stop fantasizing about my kid's nanny.

৵ ৵

"Look, Daddy! We got Jack a pink litter box

because pink is his favourite colour, and we got food and a wand with a mouse on it." Oscar flitted in and out of view of my phone screen. Probably because he was dancing around the living room and waving the wand that had a string with a toy mouse attached to it. A flash of grey fur streaked past the screen and Oscar screamed with delight before popping back into view.

"Jack likes the toys, Daddy! He grabbed the wand right out of my hand."

"That's great, buddy," I said.

"Marmalade, no!" Oscar wandered away. "That toy is for Jack."

Tess flipped her screen so it was pointed toward her. "I brought Marmalade over at lunch. I was worried she might be lonely. I hope you don't mind."

"I don't," I said. "She and Jack get along okay?"

"They do," she said with a smile. "I think her energy might be good for him. He's been really playful this afternoon."

"Thanks again for taking Oscar to pick up pet supplies."

"My pleasure. Are you sure it was okay to Facetime you? I know you're at work, but Oscar really wanted to show you the stuff we bought. He said Melody let him video call you during the day."

"It's fine," I said. There was a rap on my office door and my best friend Elliot stuck his head in. I waved him in. Instead of sitting in the chair across from my desk, Elliot joined me behind it, staring interestedly at the screen.

I ignored my immediate instinct to shield Tess from his gaze. She didn't belong to me. Trying to keep her from being seen by other single men was ridiculous and pathetic behaviour on my part.

"Hey there," Elliot said. "You must be the new nanny. I'm Elliot. Sam's boss and best friend."

"Hello," Tess said.

"He's not my boss," I said. "And if he doesn't knock it off, his status as best friend is in danger as well."

Tess laughed. Oscar climbed into her lap and peered at the screen. "Uncle Elliot! Hi!"

"Hi, big guy. How's it going?"

"I got a cat. His name is Jack. He only has one eye and three legs, and he told me he used to be a pirate's cat and helped him find his treasure."

"Wow. That's pretty cool," Elliot said.

"I know," Oscar said. "Tess, I'm hungry."

"I'll cut you up an apple," Tess said. "Say bye to your dad."

"Bye, Daddy."

"Bye, Oscar. I'll see you tonight."

Tess waved awkwardly before ending the call.

Elliot sat down in the chair across from my desk and grinned at me.

"What?" I said, even though I knew exactly what was *what*.

"She's cute. You didn't mention that when you said you'd found a new nanny for Oscar."

I shoved my phone into the inside pocket of my suit jacket and leaned back in the chair. "Just say what you want to say, Elliot."

"You gonna bang her?"

I rolled my eyes. "She's twenty-five."

"So? You're only thirty-two."

"Seven years is a big difference."

"No, it isn't," Elliot said.

"She's too young for me."

"You only think that because she's Stephanie's age, and Stephanie was a total flake."

I scowled at him. "I thought you liked Stephanie."

"I did, until she walked out on you and your kid."

I scrubbed a hand through my hair. "Which is exactly why I'm not going to date Tess. I'm not putting Oscar through that again."

"Hey, I get it." Elliot leaned forward, his hands dangling between his knees. "But I didn't ask if you were gonna *date* Tess."

"I'm not that kind of guy," I said. "And I don't think Tess is that kind of woman."

"There is nothing wrong with a friends with benefits relationship," Elliot said. "It might be the best thing for you. You've been really tense lately, Sam. Playing a few games of 'hide the bishop' will fix that."

"You're one to talk. When was the last time you had sex?" I said.

"We're not talking about me," Elliot said. "We're talking about you and you're totally obvious crush on your kid's nanny."

"Maybe we should talk about you and you're totally obvious crush on your boss," I said.

"Not the same thing," he said. "You have a chance with your crush."

"One, Tess is not my crush, and two, sooner or later Rachel is going to realize that her fiancé is a douchebag."

Elliot shrugged. "Even if she did, I still don't have a chance. She's not going to date her assistant."

"You don't know that."

Elliot stood. "Trust me, I do. I'm the one who's worked for her for three years, remember? Anyway, it would be against company policy for us to date. Considering I only got this job because of you, I'm not gonna fuck it up and lose it because I want to fuck my boss."

"Elliot," I said, "you might have got the job because of me, but you're damn good at it. Rachel would be up shit creek without you."

"Maybe. I gotta go. Later, man."

Elliot left my office. I sank back in my chair, staring out the window behind me. It was snowing again and the drive home from the city would be a bitch. Still, the thought of Tess being in my house when I got home cheered me considerably. Maybe Elliot was right, maybe a friends with benefits relationship was what I needed. I missed sex. Missed it a lot.

So, ask Tess if she's interested.

I scoffed out loud before turning back to my computer. There was no way in hell I was asking my kid's nanny if she was interested in having casual sex. She'd quit on the spot and then I'd be totally screwed.

I needed to completely forget even the idea of asking her. Tess wasn't looking for casual sex.

Chapter Five

Tess

Casual sex. That's what I needed, I decided, as I watched Oscar throw himself at Sam when he walked through the front door.

Maybe then I wouldn't be so hung up on wondering what Sam looked like naked. Maybe then I wouldn't be having mini fantasies about what it would be like to date Sam. I barely knew him and being this attracted to him already was ridiculous.

He was an amazing dad, had a killer body, and he was smart and well-spoken. Which meant his flaws probably revolved around his bedroom skills. He was probably a terrible kisser, right? Or his idea of foreplay consisted of a lick and a poke.

Maybe, but I bet his penis is straight as a ruler.

My cheeks turned bright red. I said a silent prayer of thanks that Sam was too busy listening to Oscar chatter about his day to notice my blush. It didn't matter if his dick was straight, I was never gonna see it. Technically the guy was my boss, and

I needed the money I was getting for babysitting Oscar to pay my rent. Sure, I wouldn't be homeless or anything if I didn't get the money, but the idea of spending my hard-earned savings made me cringe.

"How was your day?"

I realized Sam was speaking to me and I forced myself to concentrate on what he was saying and not how good he looked in his suit.

"It was good. We had a fun day, didn't we, Oscar?"

"Yep. We went sledding. Tess pulled me over a snowbank, and I fell off the sled," Oscar said.

I cleared my throat. "Uh, it was a small snowbank."

Sam laughed before setting Oscar on the floor. "I'm glad you had fun."

"I did." Oscar swung from Sam's hands then stood on his feet.

Tess, leave!

Shit, I was standing there like an idiot. Marmalade took that moment to walk by me, rubbing up against my legs and purring. I scooped her up. "Okay, well, good night."

"Night, Tess," Sam said.

"Daddy, I want Tess to stay for dinner," Oscar said.

"Oh, uh, I'm sure Tess has her own dinner plans..." Sam looked more uncomfortable than a cat with tape stuck to its back.

"That's right, I have my own dinner to cook," I said to Oscar.

"No, you don't," Oscar said. "You said you didn't have any food in the house. It's why you had two sandwiches at lunch because you didn't have breakfast."

Shit. Who knew that Oscar would remember everything I said to him?

"You don't have any food?" Sam was staring at me like I was Oliver Twist asking for more gruel.

"I need to go grocery shopping," I said. "But the roads have been bad and now that Roger left, cooking for one is depressing."

Nice work, Tess. Keep reminding him what a loser you are. That's sexy as hell.

Sam was still looking at me with this weird combination of pity and worry.

"Anyway, have a good night and I'll see you in the morning." Marmalade was squirming in my arms. One Eyed Jack appeared in the hallway, and I hissed out a breath when Marmalade jumped from my arms to join him, drawing blood across the palm of my left hand. Man, I really needed to trim her nails.

"Sorry," I said. I reached for Marmalade, stifling my curse when she dodged away and ran down the hallway, Jack hot on her heels.

"You're bleeding, Tess." Oscar pointed at my hand.

"Just a small scratch," I said. "Nothing to worry about. Marmalade, c'mon, kitty. Here kitty, kitty."

"Daddy, I want Tess to stay for dinner," Oscar repeated.

"I think that's a great idea," Sam said.

I stared at him, my palm stinging, and my confusion written all over my face. "I... what?"

"You should stay for dinner," Sam said. "I'm

making spaghetti. Do you like spaghetti?"

"Uh, yeah, but I don't need to stay for dinner. I can -"

"I insist. We would love it if you were our dinner guest." He picked up Oscar and flipped him upside down, letting him dangle in the air. "Wouldn't we, buddy?"

Oscar screamed laughter before waving at me. "Sgetti's my favourite, Tess. Daddy puts broccoli in it."

I stared at Sam who shrugged. "My kid is a big broccoli fan. He didn't get it from me. C'mon, what do you say? Spaghetti with broccoli. You know you're dying to try it."

He wiggled his eyebrows at me before swinging Oscar back and forth like he was a golf club. I laughed and said, "Spaghetti with broccoli, huh? How can I resist?"

"Great!" Sam set Oscar down and the kid wobbled around like he was a spin top.

"My brain feels funny now," he said.

Sam and I both laughed before Sam pointed to my bleeding palm. "I'll get you a band-aid for that."

"Thank you," I said.

He headed upstairs and Oscar followed me into the kitchen, watching as I rinsed the scratch on my palm before washing it well with soap. "Remember, little man, if Jack scratches you accidentally, you have to immediately wash the scratch with lots of soap and rinse it at least three times with water. Right?"

"Right," he said as Sam joined us in the kitchen.

He had changed into a pair of jeans and a long sleeve shirt that clung to his broad chest. "Daddy, Tess is gonna be an animal tech…tech…" he frowned in concentration, "nurse. An animal nurse."

"Oh yeah?" Sam said. He had a hand towel with him, and he blotted the scratch dry. "You're going back to school?"

"I am." My voice was unsteady, but whether that was because of how close Sam was standing to me or whether it was the scent of his aftershave, I wasn't sure. Either way, I was at least eighty percent certain that it would be inappropriate of me to bury my face in his neck and take a big old sniff.

Sam ripped open the band-aid. "When?"

"In May," I said. "I was accepted into the vet tech program at Valley College."

"Congratulations." His smile was genuine and warm. "You must be excited."

"I am," I said. "I love animals and always wanted a career working with them, but Roger was deathly allergic to cats."

"I guess now that you have Marmalade, there's no chance of the two of you getting back together, huh?" Sam's voice was casual. Maybe too casual?

"No," I said. "Zero chance."

Sam pressed the band-aid over the scratch, using his fingers to smooth the sticky ends down. I shuddered all over at the touch of his fingers against my palm. Man, this close to him, I could really see how gorgeous those blue eyes of his were. I was close enough that I could lick the faint scar I saw running across his jawline if I wanted.

Lick him! Lick him like a lollipop!

I wasn't sure if my thoughts were written across my face or what, but Sam took a step back, shoving his hands into the front pocket of his jeans and clearing his throat. "Sorry, I should have let you do that yourself. I'm used to helping Oscar with... uh, sorry."

"It's fine," I said. "I appreciate the assist."

Good God, I was a moron.

"Sorry that it's a Spiderman band-aid. It's the only kind we have," Sam said.

"Spiderman is the best superhero," Oscar said.

"So you keep saying," I said to him with a grin. "But I really feel like you haven't given Wonder Woman the proper chance yet."

Oscar just shrugged. "I'm hungry, Daddy."

"Well," Sam shoved up the sleeves on his shirt and I stared for an inappropriately long time at his weirdly sexy forearms, "let's get to making dinner then."

࿇ ࿇

Sam

"So, will you ever have broccoli in your spaghetti again?" I said.

"Don't take this the wrong way," Tess said with a grin, "but hell, no."

I laughed as I closed Oscar's door until it was only open enough for Jack to slip in and out of the room. Oscar had fallen asleep quickly for a record-breaking two nights in a row, only requiring one story from me and one story from Tess before he drifted off. Jack was curled up against his back when we turned off the light, and Tess had scooped Marmalade up before she could make herself comfortable too.

"I noticed you had quite the pile of broccoli on your plate when you were finished." Tess carried Marmalade down the stairs. I tried and failed not to stare at her perfect ass as I followed them.

"Broccoli's my least favourite cruciferous vegetable," I said.

She laughed, and my damn cock twitched in my jeans. Man, Elliot was right, I really did need to get laid if just a woman's laugh was making me hard.

Not just a woman's laugh. Tess's laugh.

"Anyway, thank you again." Tess was trying to shove her feet into her boots while holding a wiggling Marmalade. "I enjoyed dinner and the company."

"Do you want a glass of wine?" I said.

Inviting her to stay longer was stupid of me, but I couldn't resist. I wanted to spend time with her. Pure and simple.

"Sure." She set Marmalade down and the cat immediately took off down the hallway and bounded up the stairs. No doubt to join Jack on Oscar's bed.

"Great. Make yourself comfortable in the living room. I'll grab the wine."

She headed to the living room while I went to the kitchen. I ignored my inner voice telling me I was making a huge ass mistake, as I poured us both a glass of wine. When I returned to the living room, Tess was sitting on the couch, her feet tucked up under her and the flames from the gas fireplace casting shadows and light on her face.

I hesitated only briefly before joining her on the couch instead of the recliner. I handed over her glass of wine and raised mine in a toast. She raised hers and I said, "To trying spaghetti and broccoli."

She laughed and clinked her glass against mine before taking a sip. "This is good. Thank you."

"You're welcome."

We sat in surprisingly comfortable silence for a few minutes, both of us studying the Christmas tree in the corner. Oscar had helped me decorate it, which meant the ornaments were placed on it haphazardly, and the lights weren't even close to being wound evenly around it.

"I can't believe the cats haven't knocked over the tree," I said.

"I've seen them exploring it a bit, but no climbing yet," Tess said. "So, what exactly do you do for work, Sam?"

"I'm the marketing director for Valley River Outfitters."

"The outdoor clothing store?" she said.

"Yes, although we sell more than just clothing," I said. "We also sell camping supplies, hunting gear, fishing gear, mountain climbing gear, that sort of thing."

"I've never been in one of the stores," Tess said. "I'm not what you would call outdoorsy."

I laughed. "Oscar and I do a lot of camping in the summer, but I'm not a hunter and my fishing skills are abysmal."

"Do you like your job?" she said.

"Very much. I started working part time at the retail store to make some extra cash while I earned my bachelor's degree. When I finished my degree, I applied for a position with the corporate office in the marketing department. I got it and worked my way up to the director position."

"Wow." Tess was looking at me like I had solved world hunger or something. "That's really impressive."

"Thanks," I said. "Being in marketing wasn't exactly a childhood dream, but I loved it enough to pursue my master's degree in digital marketing a year after I got my bachelor's."

"You have a master's degree?"

"I do."

"Holy shit." She took a sip of wine. "Sam, considering you're only thirty-two, that's an incredible accomplishment. Your parents must be so proud of you."

I laughed. "They are."

"My mom always told me she knew I would go after my dream of working in a vet clinic. She'd be really happy that I'm doing it," Tess said. "I wish she was here to see me following my dreams."

Her face was wistful and just a little sad. I wanted to hug her, to try and comfort her in some small way. Instead, I sipped my wine and said, "Hey, if you, uh, need money, I'm happy to pay you early for babysitting Oscar."

She paused with her wine glass halfway to her mouth. "Why do you think I need money?"

My throat was suddenly dry. I took a swallow of wine. "Well, you don't have any food for starters."

"Because I haven't gone grocery shopping," she said. "Not because I don't have the money for it. Why are you assuming I'm destitute?"

"You did just get laid off from your job," I said.

"Yeah, but it's called savings, Sam," she said.

She was irritated with me. Feeling stupid and regretting I'd even brought it up, I said, "I'm sorry. I shouldn't have assumed. It's just that Mrs. Neeman told me…"

"Told you what?" She arched her eyebrow at me.

"That you were broke and couldn't make your rent and were on the verge of being homeless."

She sipped angrily at her wine. "You shouldn't believe every bit of neighbourhood gossip you hear."

"You're right, I shouldn't. I apologize," I said.

She traced the rim of her glass with her fingertip. "I'm not broke, Sam. I'm doing just fine for money. Yeah, it'll be a little tight with going back to school, but I'm in no danger of being homeless. I agreed to babysit Oscar because the more money I earn, the less I have to dip into my savings, not because I'm on the verge of starving to death."

"I know," I said. "I was being an ass."

"You weren't," she sighed. "But, man, as much as I love this neighbourhood, I sincerely hate how gossipy it is. Why can't people just live their own lives?"

"I guess because their own lives are boring," I said.

"Maybe." She finished off the last of her wine and stood up. "It's getting late, I should go."

Cursing myself for what I'd said and ruining a perfectly nice evening, I stood up too. "Right, of course. Thanks for having a glass of wine with me."

"Thanks for inviting me." She carried her wine glass to the kitchen. I trailed after her like I was Oscar, eager to spend every minute of time with her that I could.

She rinsed her glass and set it in the sink before walking to the front door. She pushed her feet into her boots and grabbed her jacket from the hook, shrugging into it. "Thank you again for dinner, Sam."

"Marmalade," I said.

"What?" She stared at me in confusion before understanding dawned. "Oh my God, I almost forgot my damn cat."

I grinned as she called Marmalade in a high-pitched baby voice that should have been annoying but was adorable. My gut was tensing with anticipation. Marmalade wouldn't leave Oscar's bed. Tess would have to go get her. Which meant walking by my bedroom.

Which meant I could casually offer to make up for my stupid assumption about her money trouble, by inviting her into my bedroom, undressing her, and eating her pussy until she came all over my face.

My cock turned to stone against my jeans and my pulse thudded in my ears. My face was too hot, and I couldn't see anything but a vision of Tess naked in my bed. That glorious curly hair of hers spread out on my pillow, her back arching, her hands digging into the sheets, and her thighs spread wide as I tasted her pussy.

"Sam?" Tess's voice was coming from a distance. I could barely hear her over my heartbeat. I had to step closer, right?

I moved in on her like a big cat stalking its prey. My hands pressed into the wall behind her, caging her in as she stared up at me. Her face registered confusion for only a couple of seconds before I saw the same need that was on mine spread across her face. Her pale skin flushed with colour and she licked her full lips as she studied my mouth.

"Sam?" she whispered.

"I feel terrible about my assumption earlier," I said. My voice was low and thick with need. Could she hear how much I wanted her? "I'd like to make it up to you."

"What did you have in mind?" Her voice was breathy and charged with its own crackle of need.

My cock was now painfully hard. I leaned down, my breath stirring the curls that were brushing against her cheek. "I was thinking maybe I could eat -"

Ten razor sharp needles sunk into my calf. I jerked away, clamping my mouth shut against my curse as Marmalade unhooked both of her paws from my denim covered calf. She sat at our feet before licking delicately at her right paw.

"Great, now she has the taste of human blood," I grumbled.

"Are you okay?" Tess was giving me a worried

look, but I could still see that intoxicating lust just below it.

I looked away, concentrating on the stinging pain in my calf and not the fact that I was still very much interested in taking Tess to my bed.

Bad idea, Sam. Very. Bad. Idea.

I took another step back, putting more space between us. Disappointment flashed across Tess's face, but she scooped up Marmalade, holding her like a shield against her body. "I should go. Right?"

"Yes," I said. "Good night, Tess."

"Night."

She opened the door and slipped out into the darkness. I stood on the porch and watched until she was safely inside her own house. My sock feet were starting to freeze and my flesh had broken out into goosebumps, but I stayed outside until my cock finally caught up to my brain and realized it wasn't going to be sinking into Tess's tight warmth anytime soon.

My mood as deflated as my dick, I stepped back inside and locked the front door before shutting off the lights and heading upstairs. I checked on Oscar, crouching next to his bed, and smoothing his hair back from his face. Jack stared at me over Oscar's narrow shoulder. His remaining eye gleamed in the light from the Spiderman nightlight plugged in next to the bed. When I reached over and petted him, he purred loudly, resting his chin on Oscar's shoulder as I scratched around his ears and the top of his head.

Oscar smiled in his sleep before mumbling,

"Good boy, Jack. Find the treasure."

I grinned and kissed his forehead. God, how I loved this kid. He was the best thing that had ever happened to me. I kissed his forehead again before heading to my own room.

Oscar is what matters, I told myself as I brushed my teeth and undressed. Not you or your horniness for Tess. Remember what's important – your kid and his happiness.

I climbed into bed and stared up at the ceiling. Yes, Oscar's happiness was important, and it was what I wanted most. So, why was I selfishly wishing that I could put a little more importance on my own happiness?

Chapter Six

Sam

"Hello, Sam."

"Hi, Janet." I wasn't surprised to see Janet sitting at the table with Tess when I got home from work Wednesday night. I'd recognized her car in the driveway. "How are you?"

"Can't complain," she said before smiling at Tess. "You'd better be careful. I might try to steal Tess away from you as a nanny. She's wonderful."

I sat down across from Tess, loosening the tie around my neck. "She is. And she's all mine so don't be getting any ideas."

Tess blushed prettily and I could feel the heat rising in my cheeks too. Even to myself I sounded possessive and weird. I cleared my throat. "Oscar won't give her up without a fight."

Janet laughed and the awkward moment passed. From upstairs, I could hear the faint sounds of Oscar giggling along with his best friend from school, Janet's son, Noah.

"So, I stopped in to ask if you had plans for this weekend," Janet said. "I know it's the weekend before Christmas, but Alan is insisting we go up to the cabin since we're spending Christmas with my folks this year and it's our only chance to go. If you don't already have plans for Oscar, do you mind if we take him with us? Noah's been missing him something fierce since school ended."

"I don't mind," I said. "But are you sure you want two six-year-olds running amok in the cabin? It's not that big."

"Tell me about it," she said with a laugh. "But I know Noah would have more fun with Oscar there. Oscar is such a good kid, we'd love it if he joined us. We'd pick him up Saturday morning and have him back to you on Sunday night. What do you say?"

"Sure, I know Oscar would love it," I said.

"Fantastic!" Janet drank the last of her tea. "Make sure you pack his snow pants. Alan was looking at the security camera feed and there's twice as much snow at the cabin. He's determined to teach the boys how to snowshoe, so Oscar's gonna need plenty of warm clothes."

"I'll make sure he has everything he needs," I said. "Thank you, Janet."

"No problem. Besides, I owe you for all the times you took Noah to swimming lessons this summer." She stood and called Noah's name. The sturdy redheaded boy appeared at the top of the stairs holding Marmalade in his arms.

"What, Mama?"

"It's time to go, honey," she said.

"I'm still playing with Oscar," Noah said as Oscar appeared next to him in his Elsa dress and holding Jack.

"I know, but it's dinner time and your father will be waiting for us. C'mon, kiddo," Janet said.

Pouting, Noah put Marmalade down and walked down the stairs. Oscar set Jack next to Marmalade and followed Noah.

"Hi, Daddy," Oscar said.

I shoved my chair back so he could climb into my lap. A thread of disquiet ran through me when he climbed into Tess's lap instead and leaned against her.

"Did you ask Mr. Black?" Noah said.

"I did," Janet said. "If Oscar wants to come to the cabin with us, he can."

"I do!" Oscar bounced on Tess's lap. "I wanna go to Noah's cabin, Daddy."

"Okay," I said.

Oscar grinned at Tess before throwing his arms around her and planting a kiss on her cheek. "I'm going to the cabin, Tess!"

"I heard, little man." Tess smiled sweetly at him and warmth overtook the unease I was feeling. It was no big deal that Oscar chose to sit with Tess. He was an affectionate kid and he liked her. That was a good thing. She was babysitting him until after the New Year. It would be awful if Oscar didn't like her.

"Okay, Noah, let's go. You'll see Oscar on Saturday," Janet said.

Tess, Oscar, and I followed them to the front door, Oscar holding on to both our hands. Janet stopped in the open doorway, studying the three of us for a moment before she took Noah's hand and waved goodbye.

I shut the door, smiling when Oscar clapped his hands excitedly. "I love Noah's cabin, Daddy."

"I know you do, bud."

Tess was putting on her boots and disappointment flashed through me. We hadn't even had the chance to talk, for me to find out how her day went and tell her how mine was.

"What are you doing, Tess?" Oscar said.

"Going home, big guy." She smiled at him and smoothed his hair back from his face. "Can you do me a favour and bring Marmalade down from upstairs?"

"Nope." That stubborn look on his face, the one that reminded me so much of his mother, appeared. "You're staying for dinner. Tell her, Daddy."

"I can't," she said.

"Do you have plans?" I said.

She hesitated and while I realized I was being nosy, I also needed to know. Did she have a date? Probably. But who went out on a date on Wednesday night? Dating was for the weekend, right?

Hey, could you act more like a senior citizen if you tried?

"No," she said, "but -"

"I know you didn't go grocery shopping last night, so unless you and Oscar went on a grocery shopping adventure today, you don't have any food in your house," I said.

"We didn't," Oscar said. "We took my library

books back and I picked out some more. Then we watched *Frozen*, and then we read, and we played Twister, and then Noah came over."

"Honey, your daddy wants to spend some time with just you and him," Tess said. "Marmalade and I need to go back to our own house now."

"Marmalade wants to stay with Jack," Oscar said.

He pointed to the top of the stairs where Marmalade and Jack were sitting together. Marmalade was grooming Jack's head, and I shrugged when Tess gave me a *say something* look.

"The cats have spoken," I said.

She laughed, letting me take her jacket from her to hang back on the hook. "Do you like porkchops?"

"I do," she said.

"Porkchop Wednesday!" Oscar crowed before dancing around. "I want apple sauce with mine, Daddy!"

"Give me five minutes to change," I said, "and then I'll get dinner started."

"Can I do something to help?" Tess said as Oscar danced into the living room singing a song about pork chops and apple sauce.

"Hmm, I've been changing my clothes all by myself since I was five, but if you really want to help…"

A delightful pink tinged her cheeks, and her smile was sexy as hell.

Telling myself to stop with the flirting already, I wasn't sure if I was relieved or disappointed when Oscar appeared in the hallway and took Tess's hand. "Daddy, can I help Tess peel the potatoes?"

I laughed. "Looks like Oscar has assigned you to potato peeling duty."

"I can handle that," she said.

She and Oscar headed back to the kitchen as, with a giant stupid grin on my face, I took the stairs two at a time.

ॐ ॐ

Tess

"Dinner was delicious, thank you," I said as we loaded the dishes into the dishwasher.

"You're welcome. Oscar, clean up your dishes please," Sam said.

Oscar brought his plate and utensils over and placed them in the dishwasher. I glanced at my watch. "Okay, well thank you again, but I should probably -"

"C'mon, Tess." Oscar took my hand and tugged me toward the living room. "It's almost time for *So You Think You Can Dance.*"

I glanced at Sam who grinned and said, "You heard the kid. It's *So You Think You Can Dance* time."

"Are you sure you're okay with me staying?" I said. I held my breath. It was stupid how much I wanted to stay but I also didn't want to horn in on Sam's time with his kid.

"Yes," Sam said. "But I should warn you now that Oscar will re-enact the dance moves for us."

"I'm a great dancer," Oscar said. "I'm gonna be a ballerina when I grow up."

"That's cool," I said. "It takes a lot of practicing."

"I know," Oscar said. "Sara at school goes to ballet class and Daddy said if I was still interested after Christmas, he would sign me up for ballerina classes too. Right, Daddy?"

"Yes," Sam said.

"I'm still interested," Oscar said.

Sam laughed. "I know. There's a beginner class starting in February. I'll enroll you in it."

"Will you come watch me in class, Tess?" Oscar took my hand. "Sara's mom watches her, but I don't have a mom to watch me. Will you do it?"

I swallowed hard and glanced at Sam. His face was a mixture of sorrow and guilt that broke my heart. I turned back to Oscar. I wasn't sure if I was doing the right thing, but there was no way I was taking away that look of hope on his sweet face by saying no.

I crouched in front of him and smoothed his hair back from his face. "I would love to come watch you at ballet class, honey."

Oscar hugged me and I patted his back. God, this kid. I was already way too attached to him.

Just him? Or his dad too?

I ignored my inner voice as Sam held out his hand to Oscar. "C'mon, buddy, we've got five minutes before the show starts. What do you say we make some popcorn?"

Oscar clapped his hands. "I want Tess to melt the butter while we make the popcorn."

"Tess, do you accept this very important butter melting quest?" Sam said.

"Put me in, Coach, I'm ready," I said.

Sam's laugh warmed me in all the right places. I grabbed the butter from the fridge as Sam opened the cupboard and helped Oscar carry the popcorn maker to the counter.

He smiled at Oscar before kissing his forehead, then gave me a quick smile that made my breath catch in my throat and my girl parts sing hallelujah.

Shit, I was in real trouble here.

෫ ෬

"Listen, you probably know this already, but you're a great dad." I followed Sam down the stairs, shamelessly staring at his ass the entire way.

"Thanks, that means a lot to me," Sam said. "I love that kid and I just want him to be happy."

"He is. He definitely is," I said. Telling myself to put my boots on and leave, I followed Sam into the kitchen instead. "He's an amazing kid."

He took a couple of wine glasses out of the cupboard and took the wine from the fridge. He poured us both a glass and handed one to me. "He is. Although, to be fair, he has been extraordinarily good about going to bed as of late. That is completely out of character for him. And you haven't yet got to witness one of his infamous meltdowns."

I laughed and then took a sip of wine. "Hmm, let's hope we avoid meltdowns until after the New Year."

Sam headed toward the living room and, like the smitten puppy I was, I followed him. The Twister mat was still spread out on the floor in front of the couch. We stepped over it and sat on the couch. Our thighs weren't touching, but we were definitely sitting closer than we were last night. Feeling like a teenage girl on her first date, I took a fortifying drink of wine and tried to act normal.

Sam sipped at his wine, before his face took on a pensive look. "He's been bringing up his mom more and more often lately. It's hard for him now that he's at school and he sees all the other kids' moms."

I took his hand and squeezed. "I'm sorry about the loss of your wife, Sam."

"Thank you. Susan and I weren't married though. We were planning on it, and then Susan got pregnant. I wanted to do a quick courthouse wedding, but she wanted to wait until after she had the baby. She said she wanted to walk down an aisle with our friends and family there, but also not be as big as a house when she did."

His hand tightened on mine. "If I'd known…" he cleared his throat. "Anyway, I just wanted to say thank you for telling Oscar you would go to his ballet class. You didn't have to do that but I'm grateful you played along."

"I wasn't just playing along," I said, hoping the hurt I felt wasn't evident in my voice. "I meant what I said. I would love to watch him at his class. Unless you don't want me to be there?"

"No, that's not it. I just don't want you to feel obligated to do something because Oscar asked you to do it."

"I don't," I said. "I am looking forward to watching Oscar dazzle the world of ballet with his sick dance moves."

Sam laughed and casually shifted closer until his thigh touched mine.

Holy crap. Was this really happening?

He stared at the Twister mat in front of us, tapping his foot on the closest red circle. "Oscar made you play Twister, huh?"

"Yeah. That kid is bendy as hell." I jumped when Marmalade came streaking into the living room, followed by Jack. She bolted over the recliner before landing with a heavy thud on the floor. Jack jumped on her and they wrestled furiously before Marmalade broke free and raced from the room. Jack chased after her, the sound of their footsteps weirdly loud in the quiet house.

"Man, for only having three legs and one eye that cat can move," I said. I licked the wine that had spilled down the side of my glass, blushing furiously when I realized Sam was watching me. "Sorry, that was rude."

He didn't reply. He was staring at my mouth and when he finally lifted his gaze to mine, the desire in his eyes turned my mouth dry and my pussy wet. Rational thought left the room and I slicked my tongue across my dry lower lip before whispering, "Sam."

He took my wine glass and set it on the side table to join his before turning to face me. His big hand slid under my hair and cupped the back of my neck. When he tugged, I came willingly forward for his kiss, resting my hand on his thigh and parting my lips in invitation.

"Tess," he breathed my name like a prayer

before he brushed his mouth against mine. It was light and gentle, and I immediately wanted more. Needed more.

His grip tightened, holding me still as he kissed me again, those same light brushes that drove me insane with need. I licked his top lip, a quick flick of my tongue, satisfied at the sound of his low groan.

When he took the kiss deeper, I wanted to shout hallelujah. Instead, I parted my lips and welcomed his tongue, stroking it with my own and encouraging him with soft sounds of need. He tasted like wine and sin and, my God, could the guy kiss.

As he teased and tormented me with small nips and licks, his free hand stroked lazy circles over my thigh. I arched my back when his hand slipped to my ribs, silently encouraging him to move higher.

Instead, he traced each of my ribs before letting his fingers trail across the underside of one breast. I groaned in frustration. He made a low chuckle before kissing down my neck.

"Sam," I moaned. "Please."

"Patience, honey," he said as his fingers stroked the hollow between my breasts.

Okay, so scratch off terrible at foreplay from his list of potential flaws.

I moved closer and tugged impatiently at the hem of his shirt, surprise and hot desire flowing through me when he lifted his arms so I could pull it over his head. I tossed it on the back of the couch and stared greedily at his gorgeous chest.

Good God, he really was in amazing shape. I

reached out and trailed my finger over his abdominal muscles, smiling when he groaned harshly.

"You're beautiful," I said.

"So are you." He kissed me again, the sweetness replaced with a hard possessiveness that heated me up to an inferno of need. He pushed me back onto the couch. I made a muffled grunt of pain when I landed on the toys Oscar had left behind.

He muttered a curse and pulled me into a sitting position. I was frantic to feel his hard length on top of me. Instead of taking the time to sweep the toys from the couch, I tugged hard on him, giggling when we rolled off the couch, landing with a heavy thud and a tangle of limbs on the slippery Twister mat.

"Shit. Are you okay?" Sam said.

I giggled again. "Yes. Are you?"

"Yes, I… oh, fuuuuck…" He groaned into my throat when I cupped his cock, my fingers stroking that heavy hardness.

It was difficult with the denim covering it to ascertain the straightness of it, but holy crap, I had no problem noticing he was bigger than Roger. I parted my legs and urged Sam to move between them. He did what I wanted, rubbing his cock against my pussy as I squeezed his narrow hips with my thighs.

We were probably a little too old to be dry humping on the floor of his living room, but I wasn't about to tell him to stop. Not when it felt this good. He cupped my breast, rubbing his thumb over my hard nipple as he kissed the curve of my jaw.

"Sam, please." I rocked against him, needing more of that delicious friction. I'd never come just from rubbing myself against a guy before, but hey, first time for everything, right?

He kissed me again, his tongue sliding deep into my mouth as we rocked harder and faster.

"I want you so much, Tess," he breathed against my mouth before sucking on my lower lip.

I moaned and clutched at his back, digging my nails into his lower back. "You keep doing that and I'm gonna come."

"Oh yeah?" His boyish grin was sexy as hell. He flicked my nipple with his thumb, making me gasp. "Maybe we should go upstairs and -"

"Daddy?"

Sam froze, staring wild-eyed at me. We hadn't turned any lights on, but I knew as well as he did that the light from the fire and from the Christmas tree were more than enough for Oscar to see what we're doing.

"What are you and Tess doing?" Oscar stood next to us and stared curiously at me.

I couldn't think of a single thing to say. My face was bright red, and my horniness had disappeared as quickly as Sam's erection.

"Um…" Sam stared frantically at me.

"Are you guys playing Twister?" Oscar said. He planted one foot on a blue circle and one on a yellow, grinning excitedly at us.

"Yes," Sam said. "Tess and I were playing Twister."

"Can I play?"

"Nope, you're supposed to be in bed," Sam said. He moved away from me, grabbing his shirt and yanking it over his head as I hopped up faster than a rabbit on crack and patted down my hair. I smiled faintly at Oscar as he stepped to a red circle.

"I wanna play Twister."

"It's bedtime. Why did you leave your bed?" Sam said.

Oscar held out his arm, showing Sam the scratch on his forearm. "Jack and Marmalade ran across my bed and scratched me. I have to wash it with soap and rinse it three times with water. Right, Tess?"

"Right," I said.

Without looking at me, Sam scooped up Oscar in his arms. "C'mon, buddy, let's go wash your scratch."

"I want Tess to wash it," Oscar said.

"She has to go home now," Sam said.

He still wasn't looking at me. Feeling stupid, I nodded when Oscar said, "Is it your bedtime too, Tess?"

"Good night, Tess," Sam said.

Rejection had never stung so much. My face red, I walked past them and shoved my boots on and grabbed my jacket. Marmalade was nowhere to be found, but I wasn't sticking around to look for her.

"Uh, is it okay if Marmalade stays the night?" I said.

"Yes, that's perfectly fine." Sam was standing near the kitchen, the look on his face suggesting I could bring a whole army of cats to his house for the night if only I would leave.

"Marmalade gets to have a sleepover!" Oscar said. "Daddy, can Tess stay for a sleepover?"

"No!" Sam nearly shouted.

Oscar put his hands over his ears. "Too loud."

"Sorry." Sam grimaced. "Tess can't stay for a sleepover."

"But I want her to." Oscar was starting to pout.

I whipped open the front door. "I really need to get home, buddy. I'll see you in the morning."

I shut the door behind me and sucked in a breath of freezing cold air before jogging across the yard to my own house. I hurried inside and shut the door, locking it and then kicking off my boots and dropping my jacket on the floor. I trudged through the dark house to my bedroom, falling onto my back on the bed and staring up at the ceiling.

Shit. I'd really screwed up.

Chapter Seven

Tess

My hope that Sam's awkwardness and discomfort would be gone, disappeared the minute he stepped into the kitchen. Carrying his leather computer bag in one hand, he dropped into the chair next to Oscar, studiously avoiding looking at me.

"Hey, buddy. How was your day?"

"Good. Do you like my painting?" Oscar was elbow deep in fingerpaints and construction paper. I had covered the table with a plastic sheet I found with his painting supplies. Sam picked at the edge of it as he studied the picture.

"It looks great," he said.

"I know. It's me at ballerina class. That's Tess watching me." He pointed to the stick like blob in the corner of the picture with a mass of brown paint on the top of it. "That's her hair. It's really big 'cause she's got big hair."

If I wasn't feeling so sick to my stomach, I would have laughed. Oscar was right, my naturally curly hair was on the large side and his attempt to recreate it in paint form was cute as hell.

But Sam's obvious discomfort with me was blotting out my ability to find joy in anything at the moment. Which was stupid because I barely knew him. But his coldness this morning when I'd arrived to babysit Oscar, and now this evening was making me feel like crying. I was attracted to Sam, hard-core attracted to him, but over the last few days, I'd started to realize just how much I *liked* him as well. He was funny and smart, and I loved spending time with him and Oscar. Knowing I'd potentially ruined our friendship was making me feel awful.

Clearing my throat, I said, "Hi, Sam. How was your day?"

"Good thanks. How was yours?" He didn't look up from Oscar's painting.

"We had a good day."

"Good, that's good," he said.

Awkward silence descended. Even Oscar must have felt the tension because he studied first me and then his dad, his little forehead furrowed.

"Well, I should get going." Hopeful but not expecting Sam to be any different after work than he was this morning, Oscar and I had taken Marmalade back to my place before I set him up with painting. Searching the house for my cat while Sam made it more than obvious that he wanted me to leave wasn't my idea of a good time.

"Okay, bye, Tess," Sam said.

"I want Tess to stay for dinner," Oscar said.

"Not tonight," Sam said. His tone made me

stand up and grab my phone from the counter, but Oscar scowled at him.

"Yes, Daddy."

"No," Sam said. "Wash your hands and put your painting on the fridge to dry."

"I can clean up the mess before I go," I said.

"No need," Sam said in a brisk tone. "We'll clean up."

"I want Tess to stay for dinner," Oscar repeated.

Sam shook his head. I swallowed hard when Oscar started to cry. "But I want her to stay. Don't be mean, Daddy."

"Don't cry, Oscar. I can stay for a bit longer," I said quickly. "I, uh, don't mind."

Sam frowned at me. "I appreciate that, but I'd like to have an evening alone with my kid."

Hurt tinged with a healthy amount of embarrassment flooded through me. "Oh of course, yes, I'm sorry. I shouldn't have… I mean… okay, bye. I'll see you tomorrow, Oscar."

He wailed louder, his hands clenching into fists as he let the painting drop on the floor. "No! No, Tess! I want you to stay!"

I hesitated, and Sam gave me an impatient look as he scooped the crying Oscar into his arms. "You should go."

I turned and nearly ran out of the kitchen, putting my boots on as Oscar's wails filled the silence. I grabbed my jacket and fled the house, hot tears sliding down my cheeks.

❧ ❦

Sam

I stared at the baby monitor sitting on the dresser in Oscar's room. I hadn't used it in years but had never bothered to remove it from his room. I glanced at the sleeping Oscar before switching the monitor on.

It was connected to my phone and I pulled up the video feed. It was pointed at Oscar's bed and I stooped down to kiss his forehead before leaving his room.

I had fucked up. Big time. Not just by having the best fucking makeout session of my life with my son's nanny, but with my actions afterward too. The look on Tess's face as she left earlier this evening was haunting me. I'd hurt her feelings by acting like an immature asshole and I needed to apologize.

I stuck my boots on and threw on a hoodie before grabbing my keys. I locked the door and checked the baby monitor video feed as I walked across our yard and into Tess's. I climbed the porch and knocked, hoping like hell she'd even open the door.

It opened only a few seconds later. Tess stared silently at me.

"Hey, Tess."

"Hello, Sam."

"Can I come in?"

She hesitated and I cleared my throat. "I only need a couple of minutes."

"Come in," she said.

I stepped inside, shutting the door behind me

and taking off my boots as Marmalade rubbed up against my legs and trilled.

I petted her before straightening to see Tess disappearing into the kitchen. I hung my jacket on the hook and followed her, my stomach churning. She was wearing a thick sweatshirt and leggings, and her long hair was in a messy bun. My stomach tightened. Her eyes were puffy with the tell-tale signs of crying.

Fuck, I was an asshole.

She sat down in a chair, picking at a container of Pad Thai from one of our local Thai restaurants. I sat down in the chair across from her, setting my phone on the table so I could see the video feed of Oscar. He hadn't moved, and both Tess and I watched as Jack jumped onto the bed and curled up against the small of Oscar's back.

"You like Thai food, huh?" I said.

"Yes."

"Me too."

"That's good." She poked at the noodles.

"I'm an asshole," I said. "I'm sorry."

"Apology accepted," she said without looking at me. "I'm sorry too."

"For what?" I couldn't figure out for the life of me why she needed to apologize.

"I overstepped," she said. "You asked me to leave and I should have left immediately."

I winced as she took a drink of water. "I offered to stay because I was upset that Oscar was upset and I wanted to help. But it was wrong of me to do that when you'd asked me to leave. So, I'm sorry."

"I shouldn't have asked you to leave," I said.

She just shrugged and continued to poke at her half-eaten noodles. Shit, this was going terribly.

I studied Oscar's sweet face before saying, "When Oscar was two, I met a woman named Stephanie. We started dating and three months later, she moved in. She was the first woman I'd dated since Susan died, and I was thrilled when Oscar liked her. I mean, he was and still is, a pretty friendly kid, but he really took to Stephanie right away. And she liked him too, you know?"

I glanced up at Tess. She was studying me silently and I made myself go on. "I knew Stephanie wanted to go to New York. Knew that she dreamed of being on Broadway. I supported her dream, I did. She was a great singer, and she deserved her chance. When she got her shot, I was happy for her. I swear it."

I looked at Tess again, hoping she believed me. Her face had softened, and she gave me a small smile. "I know you were."

"I talked to our CEO about transferring to the New York office. He was agreeable to it. I couldn't wait to tell Stephanie. I loved her and Oscar loved her, and I thought she would be thrilled that we were moving with her, but..."

I fell silent. I no longer loved Stephanie, but I still felt the sting of her rejection.

When Tess reached out, I took her hand and linked our fingers together. "I was wrong. She didn't want us moving with her. She wanted to go alone. She said I would be a distraction, and that trying to be the mother I expected her to be to Oscar and establish her singing career was too much for her."

I laughed bitterly. "I didn't handle it very well. I was angry with her and we fought. I told her I'd never expected her to be a mom to Oscar and she called me out on my bullshit."

I met Tess's gaze. "It was bullshit. I did want her to be a mom to Oscar. I felt, still feel, so guilty that he doesn't have a mom."

She squeezed my hand, giving me a look of sympathy. "It's not your fault he doesn't have a mom, honey."

My throat burning, I watched Oscar on the screen to give myself some time to collect my thoughts. "Anyway, Oscar did not take Stephanie's leaving well. He was only four and he... he didn't understand. He didn't refer to Stephanie as his mom or anything, but it was obvious that he thought of her that way. When she left, it crushed him. Hell, it crushed both of us. The first few months after she left, I had to really struggle to be present and be a good dad for Oscar. He didn't deserve that."

I swallowed hard. "I like you, Tess. I like you a lot, and obviously I am incredibly attracted to you, but my priority has to be Oscar."

"I know that," she said. "I wouldn't ask you to put me over Oscar."

"I don't think you would," I said. "That's not what I'm trying to say. He's so attached to you already. It scares me a little. You're young and you're starting your dream career. Your life could change so much in the next few years. You're just renting and who knows where you'll be even this time next year."

She frowned. "You're making a lot of assumptions about my life, Sam. No one knows where they'll be in a year. I like you too and I'd love to try dating you."

My stomach clenched. Part of me wanted to shout with happiness. Part of me wanted to practically scream yes at her. But I couldn't do that. I needed to think of Oscar. He was what mattered. His happiness.

"I'm too old for you," I said.

"No, you're not. That's just a convenient excuse," Tess said.

She was right. I needed to be completely honest with her. She deserved honesty.

"I can't," I said. "If we dated for a while and then broke up, it would devastate Oscar. I can't – *I won't* – do that to him. Not again."

"So, you're just going to shut down your own chance for happiness?" Tess said.

"He's worth it," I said.

"Yes, he is. But I think what would really make him happy is to see his dad happy," Tess said.

I squeezed her hand before releasing it. "I can't. I'm sorry, Tess. I promise I won't let what happened last night happen again."

She sighed and pushed her food aside. "Okay, no dating. But what if we just bang?"

My jaw dropped and her face reddened. "That was really crude, but you get what I'm saying."

"You want to be... friends with benefits?" I said.

"Yes."

"That's not what you really want," I said.

She shrugged. "No, but I can compromise. I'm attracted to you and you're attracted to me. Why shouldn't we have some casual and fun sex? I haven't slept with anyone since Roger and to be honest, he wasn't that great in bed, so…"

I was tempted. Christ, was I tempted. But I couldn't do it. Not to Tess. Not to me. We would both start to want more. It would be so easy to let it morph into more. To start asking Tess to stay for dinner, to spend time with Oscar, to spend time with me. And once we were on that slippery slope of emotions, it would be impossible to jump off without shattering some hearts.

"I can't," I said.

"Can't or don't want to?"

My laugh was bitter. "Believe me, I want to. But not when it isn't what you really want. It isn't fair to you, Tess."

"I'm a big girl," she said. "Maybe you should let me decide what I think is fair."

"I can't," I repeated.

She sighed. "All right."

I wanted to sit with her, wanted to stay in her warm kitchen and talk about everything and nothing. Instead I picked up my phone, stood, and tried to smile at her. "I wish things could be different, Tess."

"Thanks for being honest with me." She dragged her container of food in front of her but stared at the noodles like they were poisonous snakes. "I'll see you tomorrow morning."

Chapter Eight

Sam

"Daddy, are you mad at Tess?" Oscar was sitting on the window seat in front of the big bay window in the living room, staring out at the falling snow.

"No. Why would you think that?" I looked up from the puzzle Oscar has spread out on the coffee table. "C'mon back and finish the puzzle with me."

"Cause you wouldn't let her stay for dinner again."

"She had plans tonight," I lied. "She can't stay for dinner every night."

"I like Tess," Oscar said. "You like her too."

"I do," I said. "She's a nice person."

"Then why can't she stay for dinner every night?"

"Well, because she has her own life. She has her own friends she wants to spend time with."

"Like Penny?"

"Who's Penny?" I said.

"Tess's best friend," Oscar said.

He continued to stare out the window. I tried to distract him from the subject of Tess. "Are you excited about going to Noah's cabin tomorrow?"

"Yeah," Oscar said. "Noah said his dad is gonna teach us to snowshoe. But I'm sad because I won't get to see Tess until Monday now."

"Buddy, remember that Dad is off until Christmas. You'll see Tess after Christmas, okay?"

He turned to stare at me, his lip drawn down in a pout. "She's not coming on Monday to babysit me?"

"No, because I took the day off. We'll have lots of fun though, I promise. We'll go sledding and play, and we'll Facetime with Grandma and Grandpa. Then the next night is Christmas Eve and we'll put cookies out for Santa and carrots out for his reindeer, okay?"

Oscar grinned, cheered by the idea of Santa and his reindeer. "I'm gonna stay awake all night and watch for Santa."

I laughed. "Well, you can try, but remember that Santa likes it when kids are sleeping while he delivers his presents."

"Why?" Oscar said.

"He's shy."

"Oh." Oscar fogged up the window with his breath and drew circles through it with his finger.

"Why don't you join me, and we'll finish the puzzle before Uncle Elliot gets here."

"Uncle Elliot's already here," Oscar said. "He's talking to Tess in her driveway."

I wasn't even a little ashamed at how fast I joined Oscar at the living room window. I stared in the direction of Tess's house, jealousy making my stomach curdle. Tess, bundled up against the cold, and her snow shovel in one hand, was standing at the end of her driveway.

My so-called best friend, Elliot, was standing beside her, smiling down at her and no doubt plying her with the old Elliot charm. My jealousy intensified when Elliot said something to Tess, and she laughed.

"Oscar, what do you say we go help Tess shovel her driveway?"

"Okay!" Oscar scrambled off the window seat and I followed him to the front door. It took me less than two minutes to get the kid into his winter gear and boots. I jammed my boots on but didn't bother to put a jacket on over my hoodie. My stomach still churning, I opened the door and followed Oscar outside.

The sun had already set but there was plenty of light from the streetlights to see Elliot standing too close to Tess for my liking. I grabbed my snow shovel and clomped after Oscar who was already halfway to Tess's house.

"Hi, Uncle Elliot!" He jumped at Elliot, squealing with delight when Elliot caught him and then tossed him up into the air.

"Hey, tough guy." Elliot tossed him up once more before setting him in the crook of his arm and kissing his cheek. "How's it going?"

"Good. Are you talking to Tess?"

"I am." Elliot grinned at me. "Hey, Sam."

I gave him a *what the hell* look that he ignored before turning back to Tess. "Tess, does Sam look grumpy to you tonight?"

Tess smiled tentatively at me. "He looks fine."

The easy banter and sense of comfort between us had disappeared. I hated it, but it was my own damn fault.

"She's just saying that. You look like you got hit in the face with a snowball," Elliot said.

"What are you doing out here?" I said.

"Talking to your lovely neighbour," Elliot said with another grin.

"More like bothering her," I said. "Tess, I said I would shovel your driveway in the morning."

"I know," she said. "But the exercise is good for me."

"Uncle Elliot," Oscar said, "you wanna play Twister with me?"

"I sure do," he said. "Tess, will you be joining us for a game of Twister?"

Her face turned red and she dug her shovel into the snow. "No, I can't."

"Shame," Elliot said.

"Elliot," I said in a low voice.

He grinned at me and shifted Oscar to his other arm. "Man, I think you've gained like ten pounds of muscle since I saw you two weeks ago. I'm a little worried about our Twister game."

Oscar laughed. "I'm really good at Twister. Tess and I played today, and she fell on her butt twice. I didn't fall once."

"Is that true, Tess?" Elliot said. "Did you, in fact, fall on your butt twice during an intense game of Twister with a six-year-old?"

Tess laughed, and my jealousy grew to grinch-like levels. "Sadly, yes."

"Let's go, Elliot," I said. "It's too cold for Oscar and Tess to be standing out here."

"Right," Elliot said. "Tess, it was nice to meet you in person."

"You too, Elliot."

"I'll shovel your driveway for you in the morning," I said to Tess. "Go inside before you freeze to death."

"Sure," she said, but she stayed where she was at the end of her driveway, shovel in hand, as Elliot, Oscar, and I returned to my house. Ignoring my urge to just pick her up and carry her into her house, I shut the door and helped Oscar out of his jacket and boots.

"Buddy, why don't you go find Jack so Uncle Elliot can meet him."

"Okay!" Oscar took off up the stairs, calling for Jack.

"What the hell, Elliot?" I snapped as soon as he was out of earshot.

"What?" Elliot said.

"I want you to stay away from Tess," I said.

He shrugged out of his jacket. "Are you asking me or telling me?"

I blew my breath out in exasperation. "She's not your type, okay?"

"But she is yours. So why didn't you invite her in to hang out with us?"

"Because Oscar is already too attached to her. I'm don't want another Stephanie issue developing.

It's better if we keep some distance between her and Oscar. He likes her a lot and that could be a problem."

Elliot hung his jacket on the hook before giving me a wry look. "Is it your kid liking her that's the problem, or is it you liking her that's got your panties in a twist?"

Oscar appeared carrying Jack before I could reply. Elliot gave me one last pointed look before smiling at Oscar. "Is that cat missing an eyeball?"

"And a leg," Oscar said.

"Hard core," Elliot said.

I was tempted to open the front door and see if Tess was still standing in the driveway. Instead, I made myself follow Oscar and Elliot into the living room.

ॐ ॐ

Tess

I put the last of the groceries away before leaning against the counter. It was Saturday morning and I'd gotten up early to get groceries before the madness of last minute Christmas shoppers hit the stores.

I stared at the bag of taco chips in the pantry. I'd bought all the ingredients for my Christmas Day nachos, telling myself repeatedly that a giant pile of nachos smothered in cheese and sour cream was the perfect Christmas Day meal.

Tears pricked at my eyes. Christmas Eve nachos had been a tradition with me and my mom. God, I missed her. I'd told Penny I would be fine on my own over Christmas and every fibre of my being was regretting it now. Even the thought of being right in the thick of holiday travel was better than spending the next five days completely alone. I really wished I had more friends.

No, you wish you could spend Christmas with Sam and Oscar.

I winced. I needed to stop thinking about Sam and Oscar. What was the point? Sam had made it clear that all he wanted was a nanny for Oscar and I wouldn't beg him for more. I had some pride, right?

The doorbell rang and I knuckled away the tears that were drying on my cheeks. Crying and feeling sorry for myself was pointless. My mom was still dead, and Sam still didn't want a relationship with me. Crying about it wouldn't change facts.

I opened the door, staring in shock at Sam. "Sam? What, uh, what are you doing here?"

"I told you I would shovel your driveway." He pointed to my cleared driveway with a look of disapproval.

"I needed the exercise."

Total lie. What I needed was something to keep my mind off of the fact that I wanted to be spending the evening with him and Oscar. Shoveling heavy, wet snow had mostly worked. Until he'd shown up with Oscar in tow and acted really weird and kind of hostile toward the guy who was supposed to be his best friend.

"What are you doing?" I said when Sam stepped into my house.

He toed off his boots. A toolbox was in one

gloved hand. He set it on the floor before taking off his jacket. "Fixing your cupboard."

"What?" I followed him into my kitchen.

"Your pantry cupboard." He pointed to the pantry door leaning against the wall. "I said I would fix it, remember?"

"Right," I said.

"It's easier to do when Oscar isn't here *helping* me," he said.

I smiled a little. "Was he excited about going to the cabin this morning?"

"Bouncing off the walls." He petted Marmalade when she rubbed up against him before pulling his hoodie over his head. It dragged his t-shirt with it, and I stared with regret at his abs. It was a real shame I'd never get the chance to lick them.

"Tess?"

Embarrassed to be caught staring, I looked away hurriedly as he shoved his shirt down. "Yes?"

"I'll need your help to fix the door, if you're good with that?"

"Right, of course," I said. I joined him at the cupboard, inhaling the scent of his aftershave, and studying the stubble on his jaw. Damn, this was gonna be pure torture.

Chapter Nine

Sam

It was pure torture being this close to Tess, but even worse sitting at home by myself. Normally, on the rare occasion that Oscar stayed overnight with a friend, I enjoyed the hell out of having the house to myself. I played video games, wore nothing but my boxers, and forgone my daily workouts in favour of eating my body weight in junk food.

But now, none of my usual plans appealed to me. Not when I knew Tess was right next door. Not when I knew what it was like to touch her, to kiss her, to hear her moan my name.

I'd lasted only two hours in my too quiet house before I was showering, grabbing my toolbox, and showing up on Tess's doorstep. Fixing the pantry door was an excellent excuse to cover my need to be with her. To see her and hear her soft laugh. Things had been awkward between us and I couldn't stand that.

The pantry door was an easy fix that I dragged out for half an hour longer than necessary. I kept the topics of conversation light, trying to recapture the magical connection that I had with Tess before I'd gone and fucked it all up.

To my surprise, she played along, accepting my light teasing about her Hulk like strength, and firing back with a few gentle jabs about my abilities with power tools. God, she smelled so good and I'd had to stop myself numerous times from burying my face in her mass of soft hair and just sniffing like a damn coke addict.

"Well, I think that's it," I said. "Unless you have something else that needs fixing?"

I looked around her kitchen, praying for a loose baseboard or a crooked cupboard. Anything to keep me with her for a little longer.

"No, that's everything," Tess said.

Defeated and stupidly bummed out, I nodded. "Right, okay then. Well, I should go."

"Thank you again, Sam," Tess said.

"You're welcome."

The old hinges from the pantry door were on the floor. I bent to pick them up at the same time that Tess did, and our heads connected with a solid thump that made my eyes water. We straightened and I reached for Tess when she staggered a little. My arm slipped around her waist like it was the most natural thing in the world.

"Tess, are you okay?"

She nodded. Her eyes were watering too, and I could see a red mark already appearing on her forehead.

"Shit." I traced my fingers over the mark. "I think you're going to bruise."

"I'm okay," she said.

"I probably gave you a damn concussion," I said.

She laughed. "I doubt it.

I smoothed her gorgeous curls away from her face. God, her hair was so soft. I threaded my hand through it, tugging lightly until her face was turned up to mine. My hand tightened on her hip as I studied her beautiful dark eyes and full mouth.

"Sam," she whispered.

"Maybe I should stay," I said. "Keep an eye on you for signs of a concussion."

A faint smile crossed that perfect mouth. "Maybe you should."

I rubbed my thumb along her bottom lip, my nostrils flaring when her mouth parted. "Tess, I…"

"Have you changed your mind about this friends with benefits thing, Sam? Because if you have, I need you in my bedroom right now before I try and fuck you on the kitchen floor."

Hot desire slammed through me and I yanked Tess up against my body. One hand slid down to cup her firm ass as I dropped my mouth to hover over hers. "I've changed my mind."

"Thank fucking God," she said.

I took her mouth in a hard kiss, telling myself to be slow and gentle. But the softness of Tess's lips, the way she ground her pussy against my erection, the flick of her tongue in my mouth, seriously tested my resolve to take things slow.

She pulled away, both of us gasping for breath. "C'mon," she said, taking my hand.

I wasted no time once I was in her bedroom. I pulled her back against me, groaning when she ground her ass against my dick. I cupped her breasts, irritated by the barrier of her shirt and bra.

She arched her back, moaning softly when I kissed her throat and nipped at her shoulder through her t-shirt. She reached behind her, rubbing my cock through my jeans.

"You're wearing too many clothes," she complained.

"So are you."

She laughed and lifted her arms. I pulled her t-shirt over her head and dropped it to the floor. I fumbled with the clasp of her bra for too long. She giggled and reached for it herself. "You're not very good at this, Sam."

"It's been a long time," I said as I yanked my shirt over my head and unbuttoned my jeans. "I'm out of practice."

"How long?" She was wiggling out of her jeans and gracefully removing her socks.

Looking like a gangly stork, I pulled my socks off. "Two years."

She paused, a goddess in nothing but her panties. "Seriously?"

"Yeah." I couldn't take my gaze from her tits. They weren't fake. They were one hundred percent, gloriously real, and I couldn't wait to get my hands on them.

"Why?" She pressed a hand against my chest.

"Like I told you before, I didn't want Oscar

becoming attached again to anyone I dated, and I'm not really into the casual sex thing."

She traced her fingers across my chest. "What's changed your mind about the casual sex?"

"You," I said hoarsely. Her fingers had moved down my stomach and were currently trailing along the open waistband of my jeans. I could barely think straight. "I want you so much, Tess."

"I want you too, Sam." She smiled at me and stepped closer, pressing those amazing tits against my chest. "I'm glad you changed your mind. Do you want this to be only for the weekend?"

I swallowed hard. "How much of an asshole does it make me to say yes?"

"It doesn't," she said. "I know you're busy with work and with Oscar. I'm fine with it only being until Oscar comes back tomorrow night. I promise I won't ask for more."

The stupid thing was, I wanted to give her more. But I couldn't. Not when it could potentially blow up Oscar's world.

"Hey." Tess touched my face gently. "You still with me?"

"Yes," I said.

"We can stop," she said. "If you've changed your mind or you're not comfortable with this, we can stop. I won't be upset."

I grinned at her and pulled her in tight against me. "I appreciate that, but the last thing I want to do is stop. I just want to be absolutely sure that you're okay with this being a casual only this weekend thing."

"I am," she said. "You?"

"Yes."

"Then let's get this party started," she said with a cute grin. She unzipped my jeans and helped me tug them down. I kicked them off and she pulled on the waistband of my boxer briefs. "These too, handsome. Don't start playing shy now."

I laughed and took them off, adding them to the pile of clothes on the floor. I stood naked in front of Tess, grinning when she made a slow perusal of my entire body. "So? Do I pass inspection?"

"You certainly do." Her gaze settled on my erect cock. A bead of precum slipped out when she licked her lips. "Big and so beautifully, wondrously straight. Magnificently straight."

I cocked my head. I'd never been complimented on my straightness before. "Uh, thanks, I think?"

She glanced up at my face, a giggle bursting free of her lips. "Sorry. Roger was uh, smaller and... bent. So, your big, straight dick is really lovely."

I laughed. "You're great for my ego. It's exactly what the average sized man wants to hear... big and straight."

"I'm pretty sure you're above average," she said.

I wasn't, but who was I to argue with her assessment of my dick size? I wiggled my eyebrows at her. "Ms. Walker, if you're trying to seduce me into sleeping with you, you're doing an excellent job of it."

"Am I? Because I'm still in my underwear and we aren't even near the bed," she said.

I picked her up, making her squeal in surprise and grab my shoulders in a death grip. "Sam!"

I dropped her on the bed and stretched out on my side next to her. I leaned over and kissed her, tracing the seam of her lips with my tongue until they opened. Her hands slid into my hair and we kissed with slow and lazy brushes of our mouths and tongues. My cock was throbbing, and I pressed it against the side of her smooth thigh, trying not to groan at the contact.

Fuck, if I came all over her leg like a horny teenager, I'd never be able to look her in the eye again. I shifted my hips back, leaving a little space between our lower bodies. I traced circles in the hollow between her breasts until she grabbed my hand and pressed it against her tit.

"Sam, don't tease," she breathed against my mouth.

I kneaded the warm, pale globe, plucking at her rose coloured nipple until it was hard. She twisted on the bed and clutched at my hair. "Sam, please!"

"Patience, honey," I said. "Don't you want this to be slow and -"

"Slow next time," she said as I bent my head. "This time I want…ohhh, God…"

I licked the tip of her nipple again before sucking on it. It swelled and hardened in my mouth and she moaned again, arching her back.

When I traced the waistband of her panties, she parted her legs immediately. I kissed her, swallowing her cry of pleasure when I slipped my hand into her panties and rubbed her clit.

I lifted my head and watched her face carefully

as I experimented with how I touched her. I varied the speed and pressure of my fingers against her clit, trying to see what worked best for her. I wanted this to be perfect, wanted her to know that I was completely willing to do whatever it took for her to –

I jerked in surprise when Tess made a loud cry of pleasure and her body arched off the bed. She gripped my wrist, grinding her pussy against my hand as wetness flooded my fingers. Panting hard, she collapsed against the bed, her face flushing when she looked up at me.

"What?" she said.

"Nothing" I said. "That just happened a little… faster, than I was expecting."

She groaned with embarrassment. I leaned down and kissed the tip of her now rock-hard nipple. "I didn't mean that as a bad thing."

"It's been a long time since a man made me come without me having to give lots of… direction," she said. "I might have gotten a little carried away when I realized you didn't need my help."

I kissed along the underside of her breast. "I'm glad I could get the job done."

She laughed, then reached down and gripped my cock. My brain went blank and my hips jerked forward as I groaned loudly.

"Your turn," she said before making a little twisting motion with her wrist that almost made me come all over her fingers.

"Fuuuuck," I groaned and pulled her hand away. "I'm about to embarrass myself."

"Well, we can't have that, can we?" she said with a giggle.

I sat up, giving her a sudden look of dismay. "Shit, I don't have a condom. None at the house either. Give me fifteen minutes to run to the drugstore and -"

"Sam, I have condoms," she said with a laugh. "Relax."

"Thank Christ," I said.

She sat up and opened the nightstand drawer, pulling out a condom and handing it to me. I ripped open the packaging and rolled it on. Tess was lying on her back on the bed, a pillow under her head and an inviting smile on her face.

"You're so beautiful," I said.

"Thank you." A faint flush tinged her cheeks. She lifted her hips when I grasped the waistband of her panties.

I dragged them down, my knuckles skimming her soft skin, and tossed them over the side of the bed. She giggled, the sound dying in her throat when I bent and kissed the patch of dark curls at the top of her pussy.

"I promise I'll eat your pussy later," I said, "but right now, I really want to fuck you."

"I want that too," she said.

I knelt between her thighs and when I slid myself into her warmth, it was like coming home. I couldn't stop my groan of pleasure, couldn't stop my head from falling back, couldn't stop the two quick and erratic thrusts.

She gasped, her knees tightening around my hips. I propped myself up on my hands above her.

"I'm sorry."

"Don't be. It feels good," she said.

She bit at her bottom lip. I groaned again when she shifted slightly, and I sunk completely into her tightness. "Oh my God."

Her warmth gripped me to the very base and I had a bad feeling that I was about two minutes from coming. I took a deep breath as Tess slid her arms around my waist and rested her feet on the back of my calves.

"I don't think I'm going to last very long." I hated having to admit that, but fuck, had I ever been in a pussy as tight as Tess's?

"After two years without pussy, I'd be surprised if you did," she said.

I laughed. Tess was more open and relaxed about sex than I'd expected. I had to admit, it was an awesome surprise.

"C'mon, big guy," she said in a teasing tone. "You gonna make me wait all day for you to do something with this glorious cock?"

"No, ma'am," I said. "My cock is at your demand."

"Then fuck me," she said. Her gentle teasing was finished, and I could see fresh need blossoming on her face.

I leaned down and kissed her, pushing my tongue into her mouth as I moved with slow, deep strokes. She returned my kiss, her hands digging into my hips as she rocked up to meet each stroke.

We found our rhythm incredibly fast. There was none of the usual awkwardness of first time sex, no fumbling for right positions, or aborted attempts to match each other's pace. We were the perfect fit.

I wanted to stay slow, but the feel of Tess's slick heat around my throbbing cock, her small moans and gasps, edged me on. It wasn't long before I was moving harder and faster, driving in and out of Tess's warm and lush body.

Her hand slipped between us and she cried out when her fingertips brushed against her clit. Her pussy tightened and I groaned, thrusting in deep as she rubbed hard at her clit. When she came again and her pussy squeezed impossibly tight around me, I was finished.

I came with a loud shout, my body shaking like a leaf as I pumped in and out of Tess's warm body. She had already collapsed beneath me and I pressed a kiss to one perfect breast before easing out of her.

"Bathroom?" I said.

She pointed to the door to the right, her chest still heaving for air.

When I returned, she had pulled up the sheet and quilt and was curled on her side. I hesitated by the side of the bed. I was new to the world of casual sex. Was I supposed to leave?

Tess patted the bed behind her. "Why are you just standing there? Get in, Sam."

Relieved, I slipped into the bed and spooned her. I kissed the back of her shoulder and cupped her breast as Tess leaned into me.

"That was awesome," she said.

"Agreed," I said.

She stroked my forearm. "Can I talk you into joining me for a post-sex nap?"

"You don't have to ask me twice." I kissed her shoulder again. "Thank you, Tess."

"Hmm," she said before yawning. "Thank you, Sam. It really was amazing. I like your dick a lot."

"He likes you too," I said with a laugh.

"I could tell." She squeezed my arm and closed her eyes.

I buried my face in her soft hair, contentment and a feeling of belonging washing over me.

Chapter Ten

Tess

"You're kidding me? You don't know how to ice skate?" I dropped my slice of pizza back on the plate and wiped my hands on my napkin.

"Nope." Sam finished off his slice and drank a swallow of beer.

"You grew up here, right?" I said.

"I did."

"I thought every kid in this city knew how to ice skate. Hockey is everything here."

Sam shrugged. "My parents gave me a choice. I could take skating lessons or go to theatre camp. I chose theatre camp."

"You're a theatre nerd?" I sat up straight on the couch. Marmalade, who'd been napping on the back of it behind me, meowed irritably when my hair smacked her in the face, and jumped down.

She stalked to the window and batted the curtain aside to stare out in the darkness. It was close to five. I'd been secretly thrilled when after we'd woken up from our weirdly long nap, Sam had accepted my invitation to stay for dinner.

Sam grinned at me. "Total theatre nerd. In grade ten, I played Hamlet in our school production, and in grade twelve, I played Danny in *Grease*."

My jaw dropped. "Can you... sing?"

"Yes."

I stared at him like he was some rare and exotic new species. "I would never have guessed you'd be a theatre nerd. Why didn't you become an actor full time?"

He brushed the pizza crumbs off his lap before sitting back. "I wanted to, but I also like money and being able to afford to eat and have a roof over my head, so I went into business school instead."

"That's a real crazy shift in careers," I said.

He shrugged. "I met Susan in my senior year, and we got pretty serious, pretty quick. She was very pragmatic and practical. The idea of being married to an actor didn't appeal to her."

"So, you just gave up your dream? That doesn't seem fair," I said.

"You gave up your dream of working at a vet clinic for Roger," he pointed out.

"True, but I'm doing it now. I hate the idea that you didn't get to live your dream. Have you ever considered doing theatre now?"

"I've thought about it here and there, but with work and Oscar... there isn't a lot of time for me to do that kind of thing."

"Well, I'd be happy to babysit Oscar in the evenings if you wanted to get back into it," I said.

"The city has a pretty active theatre scene, right? My friend Penny's cousin is into it. I bet he could give you some advice or even get you an audition."

He grinned at me. "You're just determined to have everyone live out their dreams, huh?"

"No, I'm determined for you to live out your dream," I said. "Also, there may be a teeny selfish part of me that wants to see you singing and gyrating those hips in tight pants on stage as Danny from *Grease*."

He laughed. "I think my hip gyrating days are over."

"Are they? Because I thought those hips of yours were pretty fabulously loose earlier."

"Did you now?" he said with a sexy smile.

"Mmm, in fact, I wouldn't mind seeing a replay of those loose hips."

He scooted closer on the couch. "I thought you'd never ask."

"Wait," I said when he went to kiss me. "I have pizza and beer breath. It's not sexy."

"Everything about you is sexy," he said. "Besides, I have pizza and beer breath too."

"Good point." I gripped his head and kissed him hard on the mouth.

He laughed against my lips before tugging me into his lap. I straddled him, our kisses turning soft and slow. Even with the hops and pepperoni taste, I couldn't get enough of kissing him.

"You're a really great kisser," I said.

"So are you." He ran his hands up and down my bare thighs.

After we'd woken from our nap, Sam had put

his jeans back on, but I'd slipped into a cotton nightgown. I could feel his growing erection against my pussy as we kissed.

I ran my hands over his chest, loving the feel of his warm, firm skin. I kissed my way down his throat. I nibbled at his collarbone and he hissed out a breath. His hand slipped under my nightgown and skimmed up my ribs. He cupped my bare breast, teasing the nipple with his thumb.

"Let's get rid of this," he said before tugging on my nightgown.

He helped me pull it over my head, staring appreciatively at my naked body. "Fuck, your tits are incredible."

I laughed. "Thank you. You thought they were fake, didn't you?"

Red tinged his cheeks. "Maybe."

"Everyone does because they're on the larger side for my size," I said. "But I'm just naturally blessed, baby."

"Hashtag blessed," he said so solemnly that I couldn't help but laugh again.

He cupped my breasts. When he sucked on my right nipple, I threaded my hands into his hair and arched my back. God, he was so damn good at this. Every touch of his hands, every kiss and suck and lick of his mouth, set me on fire with need.

I ground my pussy against his dick, not caring that I was so wet I was probably soaking his jeans. I needed him. I needed to know if the perfection of our fucking earlier was a fluke or if this was just how it was with us.

"Sam, I need you," I said.

"Hmm," he said before teasing both my nipples with hard sucks and slow licks. "We said slow for next time, didn't we?"

"Screw slow," I said. "Slow is stupid and boring and... ohhh, right there."

He grinned up at me as he pushed two fingers into my pussy. I gripped them hard before rocking back and forth, crying out with pleasure when he angled his thumb, so it rubbed against my clit.

"Don't come," Sam said.

"I'm going to," I said and rocked a little harder.

"Not yet."

"Yes," I said.

"No." He pulled his hand out from between my thighs.

"You suck."

He kissed between my breasts. "I want you to come on my cock."

"Well then get that straight son of a bitch out here so I can," I said.

He laughed so hard I nearly fell off his lap. "The fact that you keep bringing up how straight it is, is starting to get weird."

"Listen, when you're used to trying to have sex with a candy-cane shaped penis, you come to appreciate a nice thick, straight one," I said.

"Candy cane shaped?" He was giving me a look of horror that made *me* laugh. "You're exaggerating, right?"

"I wish I was," I said. I unbuttoned and unzipped his jeans, tugging his cock out through the opening. "Hello, new friend."

He moaned when I rubbed firmly, sliding my

thumb over the tip and collecting the precum that was beading out. When I sucked my thumb clean, his fingers dug into my hips and a harsh look of need crossed his face.

"Christ, Tess. I need to fuck you right now."

"We need to go to the bedroom for a condom," I said.

He dug into his pocket, pulling out a condom. "I grabbed this from your nightstand."

"Thinking ahead, were you?" I wiggled back, balancing on his thighs as he ripped open the condom packaging.

"I might have been hoping that you'd let me fuck you on your couch. Or over your couch. Or on the kitchen table. I'm not picky," he said.

"How generous of you," I said.

He rolled the condom on and I hopped off his lap long enough for him to shove his jeans down his legs before I climbed back on. I crouched over him, moaning when he gripped the base of his dick and guided it into me.

"You're so wet," he groaned.

I sank down, gripping the back of the couch for support as I made a few experimental thrusts. "You make me this wet."

He gripped my ass hard, pumping his hips up and down as I bounced on his lap. He teased my nipples with his lips and his tongue before reaching between us and rubbing my clit.

He was perfect at it, using the right amount of pressure I needed to get off. I clung to the back of the couch and fucked him harder, throwing my head back and crying out when he rubbed faster.

This morning hadn't been a fluke or a one-off. Being with Sam was amazing. It was like our bodies knew exactly what we needed from the other and we moved together in the perfect sensual rhythm.

"Sam," I moaned, "I'm so close."

"Come on my cock, honey," he said. "I want to watch you come."

I hadn't pegged Sam for dirty talk, but I'd be lying if I said it didn't turn me on. I bounced harder and faster, crying out when Sam thrust hard and rubbed my clit with a rough urgency. The pleasure crested inside of me. I squeezed his cock hard as I came, crying his name and digging my fingers into the couch.

Sam made a hoarse shout of need, his hands clamped down on my ass, and he thrust hard into me twice more before he came with another raspy shout. He fell back on the couch, panting hard. I buried my face in his neck, kissing his sweaty skin as he stroked my back with his fingertips.

"You okay?" he said.

"Yeah. It's good with us. Isn't it, Sam?"

"It is," he agreed. "It really is."

I straightened and studied him before touching his jaw.

"What?" he said.

"Will you spend the night?" I hoped he didn't freak out. I knew this was only casual between us, but the idea of Sam being in my bed for the night was one I couldn't let go.

The look on his face had me plastering what I prayed was a fun and casual, *very casual*, smile on my face. "It's fine if you don't want to. I just thought I would offer since it's been sooo damn long since you got laid. Frankly, I feel a little sorry for you."

A smile played at his lips as he brushed my hair back from my face. "You do, huh? Sorry enough to let me bend you over your kitchen table and have my dirty way with you?"

"You could bend me over the table *and* the couch. If you think you're up for that kind of cardio," I said. "I know it's been two years."

He grinned and lightly slapped my ass, making me squeal. "I accept your challenge, Ms. Walker. But be warned, I insist on sleeping on the left side of the bed and Oscar has mentioned that I have, on occasion, snored."

"I don't think the snoring will be a problem, Mr. Black." I gave him a lingering kiss that stirred awake new desire in my belly.

"No?" He cupped my breast and nuzzled my collarbone. "Why is that?"

"Because I don't intend on letting you sleep long enough to snore."

"A sleepover without sleeping?" he said in mock surprise. "I'm definitely in."

"Good. What do you say we take this sleepover to the shower?"

"That is an excellent idea, Ms. Walker."

Chapter Eleven

Sam

"Tess, hi!" I sounded like an excited schoolboy, but I couldn't help it. Opening up my door to see Tess on my front porch holding a fabric bag in one hand, and a plate of cookies in the other hand was the best part of my day.

Not that it'd been that long since I'd seen her. I had left her place around ten this morning. I needed to feed Jack and I'd made plans to have lunch with Elliot. Truthfully, I hadn't wanted to leave. I'd wanted to stay right where I was in Tess's warm bed. But there was this stupid idea in my head that if I'd cancelled on Elliot to spend the day with Tess, it would somehow confirm my suspicion that what was happening between us was more than casual.

My growing belief that it could be more than casual was niggling away at the back of my skull, no matter how hard I tried to ignore it. I couldn't ignore it though. Not when it was this perfect between us.

"Hi there." She smiled at me. "I know Oscar is coming home later today, but I thought maybe you'd have time to watch a movie with me. I made some peppermint chocolate chip cookies as a bribe."

I laughed. "You didn't need to bribe me. I would love to watch a movie. Come on in."

As I ushered Tess into the house, the flash of light from Sheila Kirkman's binoculars nearly blinded me.

I smiled and waved, my smile broadening when the curtain dropped, and Sheila disappeared from view. Tess and I were, no doubt, the talk of the neighbourhood, but I didn't care.

Tess might.

Unease swirled in my stomach. I closed the door and locked it, turning to face Tess who immediately said, "What's wrong?"

"Sheila Kirkman was watching us. We're the neighbourhood gossip. Does that bother you?"

"No," she said. "But if it bothers you, I can -"

"It doesn't," I said. "I just wanted to check in with you."

She shrugged. "I don't care if they gossip about us. We're both grown adults and two grown adults having casual sex is not scandalous. Even if Sheila thinks it is."

I took her jacket and hung it on the hook. "Agreed. How was your day?"

"Good. I ran an errand, did some laundry, and made the cookies. How was your lunch with Elliot?"

"It was good. He's headed to Puerto Rico on the redeye tonight. He's going to spend Christmas with his feet in the sand and a margarita in his hand."

She laughed. "Good for him. Is he dating anyone?"

"No," I said. Was Tess interested in him? Irrational jealousy was eating at my insides. "But he's in love with his boss, Rachel. He's not, uh, emotionally available."

But he's available for casual sex. You've told Tess that it's just this weekend for the two of you. Maybe she's interested in hooking up with Elliot once you two are finished.

"Are you interested in Elliot?" I blurted.

Smooth, asshole. Real smooth.

"What? No, not at all. I mean, he seems like a nice guy, but I'm not - I mean, I don't really know him that well and if he's in love with his boss…"

"He is," I said. "Ridiculously in love with her."

"She's not interested in him?" Tess said.

"She has a fiancé," I said.

"Ouch. Poor Elliot. I feel for the guy." Tess headed to the kitchen. I followed her, watching as she put the cookies on the table. "What time does Oscar get home?"

"Janet texted me this morning. They should be back around seven."

She glanced at her watch. "Perfect. That gives us time to watch the movie and maybe do some… other stuff, too."

Her sexy little smile made me want to suggest we forget the movie watching and just go straight to the other stuff.

Instead, I took a cookie when she offered it to me and took a big bite. "This is delicious."

"Thanks. I'm glad you like them." She pulled her computer out of the fabric bag. "Do you want to watch the movie in the living room or in your bedroom."

"Bedroom," I said. "More comfortable."

She grinned at me and we walked upstairs. Stupidly, I wanted to grab her hand and hold it.

You don't hold the hand of your casual sex partner, idiot.

She climbed into my bed – God, she looked so right in it – and leaned against the headboard, propping the pillow behind her back. She patted the spot beside her, and I joined her, making myself comfortable as she started her laptop and opened Netflix.

"Ready?" she said.

"I am."

I laughed when she clicked on the movie. "Oh my God, Tess."

"What?" she said with an innocent smile as the opening music for *Grease* started. "I thought you'd love this movie."

I laughed and couldn't resist putting my arm around her. She snuggled in, resting her head on my shoulder and her hand on my thigh.

"You're right" I said. "I love this movie."

෭෬ ෬

Tess

"Oh fuck, oh, Sam… please," I moaned. "Please."

He smiled up at me. "Not yet, honey."

I gritted my teeth and clamped my hands around the sheets. Sam was trying to kill me. Death by edging was a thing, right? It was totally a thing.

I took a deep breath. We'd started off strong with the movie, but by the time Stockard Channing was singing *Look at Me, I'm Sandra Dee*, my shirt and my bra were lying on the floor and Sam was sucking on my nipples.

And by the time John Travolta and the gang were gyrating their hips to *Greased Lightnin'*, my pants and underwear had magically disappeared, and Sam's face was buried between my thighs.

"Sam, I can't wait!" I pulled on his hair, not even feeling a little guilty when he winced.

"You can." He licked my clit with agonizing slowness. I bucked my hips, trying to force him to lick harder, longer.

I'd mostly lost track of time but I knew for a damn fact that it had to have been at least half an hour since Sam had stretched out between my thighs and started eating me out.

"Sam!" My voice was slightly hysterical, but could you blame me? I'd gone from a man who basically thought foreplay was a lick and a squeeze, to a man who I was starting to worry could eat a pussy for hours without letting a woman come.

"I want to make sure you're ready for me, honey."

"I'm ready! I'm so damn ready." I twisted on the bed, my hands squeezing his skull as he licked my clit again and the ache in my stomach rose to a feverish pitch. "Please!"

His thumbs parted the lips of my pussy and then, oh, bless all that was holy and light, his lips fastened around my throbbing clit and he sucked hard. Not even caring that it was loud enough for nosy Sheila Kirkman to hear, I screamed and came like a damn fire hydrant. The pleasure went on and on, Sam's tongue licking me clean as I spasmed and shook, my pussy gripping uselessly around nothing.

When he lifted his head, wiping his face on the sheet and reaching for a condom, I was still shaking and moaning and twitching with pleasure. He rolled the condom on before rubbing my inner thighs with his warm hands.

He leaned over me, his cock probing at my entrance, the smile on his face warm and inviting and perfect. "You ready for me, honey?"

"Hmm," I said, arching up when he slid into me with one slow thrust. I clenched around him, cupping his face and drawing him down for a lingering kiss. I could taste myself on his lips, and I licked his upper lip before sucking on his bottom one.

"You're so sexy," he moaned when I released his mouth.

"So are you. Fuck me, Sam."

"Yes, Tess." He dropped down on me, hooking his arms under my shoulders and holding me tight as we moved together in a slow rhythm. I closed my eyes, meeting each of his thrusts as his warm breath panted in my ear.

"Tess, look at me."

I shook my head, and he kissed my mouth. "Open your eyes, honey."

I opened my eyes, staring up into the gorgeous ocean-blue of his gaze, transfixed by the emotion and affection I could see in them.

"You're so beautiful, honey," he whispered.

I wrapped my arms around him and moved faster, squeezing my pussy around his cock, trying desperately to make him lose control. I needed him to come, needed him to finish, before I fooled myself into thinking this could be something more than just casual sex.

"Slow," he groaned. "Honey, slow."

"No." I squeezed around him again and nipped at his throat. "I want you to come, Sam. Please."

He groaned again and moved harder and faster until, with a low moan, he came inside of me. I wrapped my limbs around him as he buried his face in my throat. He was heavy, but I clung to him tightly when he tried to move.

"Not yet," I whispered.

He kissed my throat and stroked my side as I stared up at the ceiling and blinked back the hot tears. He couldn't see me crying, I wouldn't let him see how much I regretted agreeing to this weekend only with him. I'd made a terrible mistake thinking that I could have casual sex with Sam and not want more, but I wouldn't make him feel guilty about it.

It wasn't his fault I was falling in love with him.

❧ ❦

Sam

"Tess, are you sure you're okay?" I took her hand.

She squeezed it before smiling at me. "I am."

She didn't look okay. She looked tired and sad and she'd been unusually quiet the last hour or so.

"You don't have to leave yet. Oscar won't be back for another hour or so," I said.

"I know," she said, "but Marmalade has been alone all afternoon and I'm sure you want some alone time before Oscar comes home."

I didn't want that, but saying it would give her the impression that I wanted more than just casual sex.

You do, you asshole.

I ignored my inner voice as Tess grabbed the fabric bag from the kitchen table. She stared uncertainly at me. "I bought Oscar a Christmas present."

She brought out a wrapped box and set it on the table.

I smiled at her. "That was very thoughtful. Thank you, Tess."

"I bought you one too. I know this is just a casual thing between us," she said hastily, "so don't freak out that I'm thinking this is more than it is, but I saw it when I was running my errands and couldn't resist."

She set a second wrapped box next to Oscar's. My chest tightened and I couldn't help the big stupid grin that crossed my face. "You bought me a gift?"

"Yeah," she said in obvious relief at my smile. "It's nothing big or special or, uh… wait, that didn't come out right."

I laughed and leaned down to press a kiss against her mouth. "Thank you, Tess."

"You're welcome. Anyway," she glanced at her watch, "I better get going. This has been a really great weekend, Sam. Thank you."

I cleared my throat. "Thank you. I, uh, I had a lot of fun."

Idiot!

"Me too." She headed to the front door and as she put on her boots and grabbed her jacket, I was almost overwhelmed by the urge to ask her to stay. To ask her to spend Christmas with me and Oscar. But that was a stupid idea. She would have plans for Christmas already, and Tess spending Christmas Day with us would definitely give Oscar the wrong idea. I needed to stick to the original plan and not muddy the waters for any of us, despite how much I was regretting this casual sex weekend agreement.

"Okay, well, Merry Christmas, Sam. I'll see you on the twenty-seventh," she said.

"Merry Christmas, Tess."

After an awkward moment, we hugged. I buried my face in her hair and inhaled deeply. She rubbed my back and kissed my neck before breaking the hug.

"Bye, Sam."

"Bye, Tess."

She stepped outside and I stood on the porch, watching her walk across the yard to her house. I bit back my still overwhelming desire to chase after her and ask her to at least stay until Oscar got home. She didn't want to stay, and I wouldn't make her feel guilty about her decision to leave.

It wasn't her fault I was falling in love with her.

Chapter Twelve

Sam

I stared at the ceiling of my bedroom. It was after eleven and I'd been tossing and turning for the last two hours. I sat up and grabbed my phone, scrolling aimlessly through Facebook.

Today was a good day, I told myself. Just because you didn't see Tess once, doesn't make it a bad day.

I wanted to believe that, *wanted* to remember that the day with Oscar really had been awesome, but I missed Tess. Missed her at a level that should have made me nervous, but just made me depressed.

"Your day was good," I muttered to myself before pulling up Tess's contact info on my phone.

Don't do it, Sam. Don't you dare. You can't give her what she wants so don't give her hope that you can.

I ignored my inner voice and called Tess. She was my friend, right? There was nothing wrong with calling a friend to see how their day went. I wasn't calling because I missed the sound of her sweet voice.

Her phone rang and rang in my ear. I was starting to sweat a little. I hadn't seen Tess all day, not even after the snow finally stopped and I'd bundled Oscar up and we shoveled her driveway. There wasn't even a glimpse of her at the window.

Maybe she's with another guy. Maybe she's found someone else who isn't refusing to date her.

My stomach churned and jealousy seeped into the lining like bitter acid. I knew Tess wasn't dating someone else yet, but what would I do when she did? She spent a lot of time gardening in her back yard in the summer. What would I do the first time I looked over our shared fence and saw her living her life with her new man?

Hang up the phone, Sam. She's avoiding your call. Or she's sleeping. It's after eleven, you idiot.

Shit, what was I thinking? I didn't even know if Tess was a night owl like me or –

"Hello?" Her voice wasn't sleepy, but it was rushed and a little breathless.

"Uh, hi, it's me. Uh, Sam."

Smooth, asshole.

"Hi. What's wrong? Is Oscar okay?"

If I hadn't already been starting to fall in love with her, that would have done it for me. That her first reaction was concern for Oscar made my heart go into freefall.

"He's good. He's sleeping."

"Did he have fun at the cabin?"

"He did. There was a small fire at the shed of

the neighbour's place and firefighters were called to put it out. So, now he wants to be a firefighter when he grows up. Although he assures me that I should still sign up him up for ballet classes because he's going to be a ballerina on the weekends."

She laughed and the loneliness I'd felt all day finally disappeared.

"How was your day?" I said.

"Fine. Quiet. Thank you for shoveling my driveway again."

"You're welcome."

There was awkward silence and I'm ashamed to admit that my cock went half-hard when I heard the squeak of Tess's mattress.

Asshole. She was probably sleeping, and you woke her up.

"I'm sorry I called so late. Did I wake you?" I said.

"No. I'm a bit of a night owl so normally don't go to bed until around midnight. I was having a bath when you called."

I went from half-mast to fully hard. I shifted on my bed, ignoring my urge to rub my cock. "Sorry to interrupt your bath."

"You didn't. I was just getting out of the tub, but my phone was in the bedroom, so I had to make a mad, dripping wet dash for it." She laughed again but all I could concentrate on was the idea that she might still be wet and naked.

"Are you still wet?" My voice had gone rough and low.

"A little," her voice was husky. I could hear the same need in it that was in mine.

129

"Only a little? That's a shame."

She didn't reply and I said, "I missed you today, Tess."

She sighed. "I missed you too."

I needed to say good night and hang up the phone. I'd told Tess that I'd wanted it to be the weekend only, yet here I was hoping for... hell, I didn't even know what I was hoping for. I just missed her.

"Tess, I -"

"Can I ask you a question, Sam?" Her voice turned serious, and my heart dropped to my stomach. Now she would ask me what kind of game I thought I was playing with her, and I had no answer for her. No answer at all.

"Yes," I said.

"Do you think mutual masturbation over the phone would violate our weekend only casual sex agreement?"

"I... what?"

"I say no, but I'm willing to listen to your counter argument."

A smile spread across my face. "Actually, I think you'll find my counter argument pretty strong."

"Oh yeah?"

"I would argue that while mutual masturbation over the phone is not a violation, we did miss out on Friday night for our casual sex weekend agreement. I would put forward the idea that tonight, despite being a Monday and clearly not the weekend, could, in fact, be a substitute for the missed Friday evening of our casual sex weekend."

"You make a fair point," she said.

"You should probably join me in my bedroom so I can present the rest of my case in person," I said.

"Hmm, being in your bedroom would make it easier to suck your cock," Tess said.

A blizzard couldn't have stopped me from fisting my own cock at her words.

"Tess," I said hoarsely as I stroked myself from root to tip. "Get over here, right now."

She laughed. "I'll be right there."

I ended the call and slid out of bed, throwing on my robe before I checked on Oscar. He was sleeping soundly with Jack curled up against his back. I kissed his forehead before walking quietly downstairs. I unlocked the front door and opened it, not caring that the cold was turning my toes numb. Tess was already halfway across her yard. I smiled at her as she climbed my porch steps.

"Good evening, Ms. Walker."

"Hello, Mr. Black. Lovely night, isn't it?"

"Hmm," I said. I pulled her into the house and locked the door behind her before crowding her up against the wall.

She put her arms around me, gasping when I ground my cock against her and dipped my head to kiss her throat.

"You smell so good," I said. Her skin was still warm and damp despite her trek in the cold. I unzipped her jacket and cupped her braless tits through her tank top, kneading them roughly as I took her mouth in a hard kiss.

She returned my kiss, sliding her hands inside

my robe to stroke my chest and my stomach before moving to grip my cock. I sucked in a breath, muffling my groan of pleasure as she stroked me with her soft hand.

She smiled up at me. "Maybe we should take this upstairs before I drop to my knees right here and start sucking."

"Fuck," I muttered. "You're torturing me, Tess."

She smiled up at me as she kicked off her boots. 'Honey, I haven't even started torturing you yet."

She dropped her coat and not caring what it looked like to her, I took her hand and walked upstairs with her. After over twenty-four hours of not seeing her, I needed to touch her. I ushered her into my bedroom and shut the door, locking it behind us.

"We'll need to be quiet," I said. "Oscar isn't a light sleeper, but he doesn't sleep the sleep of the dead either. I'm sorry."

She frowned. "You don't need to apologize. I want what's best for Oscar too."

She truly did, I had no doubt of that. My love for Tess was becoming a steady flame. I could get lost in this woman.

She sat down on the side of the bed and crooked her finger at me. "I know I said knees, but do you mind if I sit on the bed? Hardwood is killer on the knees."

"Honey, we can be in whatever position you want. I'm not gonna complain," I said with a laugh as I joined her at the bed.

"Team player," she said as she pulled open the

ties on my robe. "I like that."

I shrugged off my robe, letting it fall to the floor as I stared down at Tess. She was mouth level with my cock and the urge to just push forward, to slide my cock past those perfect lips was overwhelming.

I closed my eyes, my head falling back when Tess gripped the base of my cock. "Oh God, Tess, please…"

She giggled softly. "Begging already, Sam? I haven't even started."

I cried out when her warm mouth slid over the head of my cock. She immediately stopped, lifting her head to stare up at me. "Hey… quiet, remember?"

"Fuck," I said in a low, desperate voice, "I'm not sure I can be quiet."

"I get it," she said with a small grin. "You haven't had this delicious tasting cock sucked in two years. But if you're not quiet, I'll have to tie you to the bed and gag you with a tie or something. Is that what you want, Sam? To be tied to the bed and gagged?"

"Maybe tomorrow night," I moaned as she stroked my dick. "Tess, your mouth. I need it."

"I know," she said before licking my cock like it was a fucking ice cream cone. "But be quiet, Sam. If you wake up Oscar and we have to stop, I really will tie you to the damn bed."

I clamped my mouth shut around my fresh groan of pleasure when Tess sucked on just the head of my dick. I threaded my hands into Tess's soft hair, holding tight as I pumped my hips slowly.

"This okay?" I rasped quietly.

She stared up at me, her beautiful mouth full of my cock, the dim light of the lamp leaving one side of her face in shadows.

"Mmhmm," she said around my dick and sucked hard.

I breathed a litany of curses before pulling her hair back in a loose ponytail. I watched as Tess bobbed her head up and down. Her soft little tongue worked the shaft, and her warm fingers cupped my heavy balls with infinite gentleness. When she pressed the smooth spot just behind my sack, I jerked forward, the pleasure so strong that I almost came right then and there.

"Fuuuuck," I breathed. "Oh fuck, Tess."

She released my cock with a soft pop and cleaned off the precum from the head with her perfect pink tongue. "You taste good, Sam."

"Take off your shirt," I said.

She pulled her tank top over her head. I immediately cupped both her tits, rubbing her nipples with my thumbs as she sucked on my cock.

I let my head fall back again, my eyes closing, as my world shrunk to just the feel of Tess's hot wet mouth surrounding my dick. I was making low grunts and moans of pleasure, my fingers tugging and pulling at Tess's nipples.

When her rhythm faltered, I opened my eyes and stared down at her. Fresh new lust roared through me. Tess had one hand shoved down her pants and was rubbing furiously at her clit.

Watching her touch herself made my desire to come in her mouth turn to an undeniable need to fuck her. I pulled free of her mouth, shaking my head when she tried to take me back.

"Wait, honey."

"What's wrong?" She stared up at me, her mouth red and swollen.

I bent down and kissed her mouth, tasting myself on her lips. It made fresh precum leak from my cock and my desire to fuck her became almost unbearable.

"Nothing," I said. "I want to fuck you."

"I want that too," she said.

"Good. Lose the pants and get on your hands and knees on the bed."

She stood and pressed another kiss against my mouth. "Whatever you say, Mr. Black."

"Shit!" I snapped.

"What?"

"No condom. Fuck, I'm so -"

She produced a condom from the pocket of her yoga pants and waved it at me.

"Thank Christ." I tore open the condom and rolled it onto my dick as she turned around and took her yoga pants off.

Jesus, no panties.

She wiggled her bare ass before climbing onto the bed and kneeling on her hands and knees. She spread her legs, presenting her little pink pussy to me. "Well? I'm waiting for that fucking you promised me."

"In a minute," I said. There was no fucking way she could show me her glistening wet pussy like that and not expect me to give it a thorough cleaning with my tongue.

She pouted at me over her shoulder. "Sam, you

said you would… oh my God!"

Her back arched and her hands dug into the sheets as I bent and licked her wet slit.

"Sam!" She moaned in a quiet voice. "Sam, oh please."

She arched her back like a cat, practically shoving her pussy into my mouth when I licked it again. I gripped her ass and used my thumbs to spread apart her pussy. I tongued her tight entrance before licking my way to her clit. I gave it a hard, firm suck, loving the way she immediately dropped her upper half to the bed, burying her face in the quilt to muffle her cries of ecstasy.

I cleaned away all of her sweet cream before straightening and kneeling on the bed between her legs. I gripped her ass again, pressing the tip of my cock against her and groaning quietly when the head slipped in and she clamped down around it.

"So tight, honey." I rubbed her lower back. "Relax for me."

She made a muffled sound of pleasure but her little pussy stayed clamped around me. I rubbed her lower back and then the back of her thighs. "Relax, honey. Let me in."

Her pussy loosened a little and I slid all the way in, my heavy balls slapping up against her pussy. This was one of my favourite positions. I loved the control it gave me, how deep I could go, and the bird's eye view of Tess's pussy swallowing my cock. I really wasn't larger than average, but if her casual hints that her previous boyfriend was small were true, then she probably felt a little apprehensive in this position.

I smoothed a gentle hand over her ass, giving her time to get used to my dick even though I really wanted to fuck her hard. "Okay?"

"Yes," she rose to her hands, tossing her hair out of her face, "it just feels like a lot in this position."

"You look so beautiful," I said. "Your little pussy fits my cock perfectly."

She shuddered around me, her pussy tightening. "God, I love your filthy mouth."

I grinned and leaned forward to cup her tits, giving them a squeeze before I straightened and pressed on her middle back. "Back down to the mattress. I want the perfect view of your pussy while I'm fucking you."

She groaned and pressed her face and upper body to the mattress again. I stroked her ass before gripping her cheeks and spreading them apart. I fucked her slowly, giving her the length of my cock a little at a time as she moaned and squirmed beneath me.

I quickened my rhythm for a few seconds, giving her some hard, rough thrusts while I reached under her and rubbed her clit with my fingers. She buried her face in the quilt again, making muffled cries of pleasure as her pussy tightened again.

I stopped before she could come, smiling when she whipped her head around and glared at me. "Sam, don't stop!"

"Shh, honey." I rocked my hips a little, making small thrusts as I rubbed her ass. I spread her cheeks and ran my thumb over her puckered hole.

She jerked and stared wide-eyed at me.

"Have you been fucked in the ass before, Tess?"

She shook her head, moaning a little when I applied soft pressure.

"I want to fuck it," I said. "Very much."

"Maybe tomorrow night," she gasped out.

I laughed and cupped my hands around her hips, holding her firmly as I started a deep and hard rhythm of fucking. "Team player, I like that."

She reached back, curling her fingers around my wrist as I fucked her.

"Touch yourself," I demanded. "Rub your clit until you come, honey."

She didn't need to be told twice. She shoved her hand beneath her, burying her face in her arm and moaning repeatedly as she rubbed at her clit. Her pussy tightened like a vice and she came hard around my dick, her inner muscles squeezing and rippling and driving me mad.

As the last of her orgasm flowed through her, I fucked her roughly, driving in and out of her wet pussy. The loud wet sounds of our coupling fueled my desire into a wild and out-of-control flame.

I had enough sense left to clamp one hand over my mouth, muffling my shout of pleasure as I drove deep one final time and came so hard, I saw fucking stars. My breath sawing in and out of my lungs, my pulse thudding in my ears, I collapsed on top of Tess.

She made a soft 'oof' as her legs gave out and she landed face first on the bed. I rolled off of her, pinching the condom closed so I wouldn't lose the damn thing. My hands shaking, I disposed of it in the wastebasket beside the bed before falling back onto the mattress beside Tess again.

"Holy fuck," I said.

"Hmm," she said.

I brushed her hair away from her face as she snuggled in, slinging one arm and a leg over my body. I stroked her side and her hip before kissing her forehead. "You good? I didn't hurt you, did I?"

"No, not at all," she said. "Thank you, Sam."

"Thank you," I said.

We laid on the bed in comfortable silence. For the first time all day I was truly content. Tess in my bed, her soft breath on my chest, and her warm body pressed up against mine, was the perfect way to end the day. I could have stayed like this forever.

To my dismay, it was less than ten minutes before Tess sat up. I sat up too, catching her arm when she reached over the side of the bed for her pants. "Stay the night."

She smiled at me, but my breath caught at the sadness in it. "Thank you, but I can't."

"You can," I said. "The door is locked, and Oscar knows to knock first."

She touched my face. "I can't, Sam. What if he sees me leaving in the morning? How will we explain that?"

"I'll set my alarm for early," I said. "He's a night owl like me. He won't be up before eight."

She hesitated before shaking her head. "I can't. I'm sorry. I don't want to take the risk, not when this is it for us."

Feeling sick to my stomach, I nodded. "Yeah, okay, I get it."

"I don't mean to upset you," she said.

"It's fine. You're right," I said. "It isn't a good idea for you to stay the night."

I climbed out of bed, putting on my robe as Tess dressed quickly. We walked silently down the stairs, neither of us speaking as Tess put on her boots and her coat.

She gave me a hesitant look, relief crossing her face when I pulled her into my arms and hugged her tight. We kissed, a slow lingering one that was tender and raw and made my throat tight.

When Tess pulled away, her eyes were bright with unshed tears, but she smiled up at me. "Thank you, Sam. I won't ever forget how wonderful this weekend was."

"Me either," I said hoarsely.

She gave me one brief, final kiss before opening the door and stepping out into the cold. I stood on the porch in my bare feet. The cold turned them numb and my body broke out into goosebumps, but I stayed where I was, watching Tess until she stepped inside her own house.

I was doing the right thing for Oscar, so why the hell did it feel so wrong?

Chapter Thirteen

Sam

"Daddy!"

I set my mug on the coffee table as Oscar ran into the living room. "What's wrong, buddy?"

He climbed into my lap, his eyes wide. "I ate the last of the carrots yesterday."

"Okay," I said. "That's fine."

"But it's Christmas Eve and we don't have any to leave out for Santa's reindeer tonight!" Oscar wailed. "They're gonna starve, Daddy!"

I kissed his forehead. "Well, we can't have that, can we? I guess we'd better run out to the store and get some more."

"Yay!" Oscar clapped his hands and danced around the room. "I'm gonna wear my Elsa crown to the grocery store."

"Sure," I said, "but you'll have to wear it over your hat. It's too cold for you to go bareheaded. Hey, what do you think about stopping at another store and getting Tess a present for Christmas too?"

"Okay," Oscar said. "Are we getting her a Spiderman shirt like mine?"

"I had something else in mind," I said. "Go get your crown while I find your hat and mittens."

Oscar ran out of the room and I headed to the front door. After Tess left last night, I'd barely slept. I'd laid in my empty bed, staring at the ceiling and wishing that Tess was still with me. I'd hit on the idea of a gift for her just before five this morning. Now I was as eager as a kid to buy it for her.

I wouldn't be able to give her the gift until the twenty-seventh, she was probably already starting her own Christmas celebration and I wouldn't intrude on that, but I couldn't wait to see her face when she opened it.

"C'mon, Oscar," I hollered up the stairs.

"I'm coming! Hold your horses, Daddy," he hollered back.

I laughed hard, stooping to pet Jack when he ambled down the stairs. "Maybe we'll even stop and pick you up some new catnip toys, old man."

He purred and rubbed against my leg before heading to his food dish in the kitchen. Oscar tramped down the stairs, holding his crown in one pudgy hand. "I'm ready, Daddy."

"Okay, kid." I took his hand and squeezed. "Let's go brave the madness that is Christmas Eve shopping."

☙ ❧

"You got Tess a really weird gift, Daddy."

Sitting on his knees on the kitchen chair, Oscar watched as I finished wrapping Tess's gift.

"I think she'll like it," I said. "Remember, she's going to be an animal nurse."

"I guess." He slurped at his mug of hot chocolate. "Can we give it to her right now?"

"No, buddy. We'll give it to her on Friday when she comes over to babysit you again."

"But that's after Christmas," he said with a frown. "It's supposed to be a Christmas present."

"I know, but Tess is busy with her friends for Christmas," I said. "We don't want to bother her."

"No, she isn't." Oscar slid his hand into the open bag of mini marshmallows and grabbed five more, letting them plunk into his hot chocolate one by one.

"No, she isn't, what?" I said.

"With her friends." Oscar poked at the marshmallows with the tip of his finger.

"How do you know that?" I set the present aside, a bad feeling starting to brew in my stomach.

"I asked her before," Oscar said. "She said she was celebrating Christmas by herself because her mommy died like my mommy did, and her friends were going away. She said she was making nachos for Christmas because she and her mommy used to made nachos on Christmas Eve. Can we have nachos for dinner, Daddy?"

The sick feeling spread through my entire body, mixed with a healthy dose of shame. I'd never even bothered to ask Tess what she was doing for Christmas, never even gave a single thought to confirming she wouldn't be alone.

"Daddy?" Oscar touched my arm. "Can we make nachos for dinner?"

"Yes," I said. "We can. You, me, and Tess."

Oscar's face lit up. "Tess too?"

"Yes," I said. "Put your boots on, buddy. We're going over to Tess's place for a minute."

❧ ❧

Tess

"I am feeling very sorry for myself, Marmalade." I smoothed her soft fur down along her spine with my fingertips as she purred and stood on my chest. I winced when she kneaded but didn't push her away.

I was lying on the couch and when Marmalade laid down, I pulled the blanket up until it covered her too. "Like, get drunk on tequila sorry for myself."

I stared out the living room window. Getting drunk was tempting but I really didn't want to spend Christmas alone *and* with a hangover. I was already going to be depressed enough. A splitting headache and an upset stomach wouldn't help.

"Maybe tomorrow, we'll just stay in bed all day and watch movies about girls who aren't nearly as unlucky in love as me. What do you say, Marmalicious? Would you like that? I mean, if I can't have the man of my dreams, I might as well watch other women get theirs, right?"

Marmalade trilled softly and butted her head against mine.

"Good point," I said. "It won't make me feel

better. Horror marathon it is. Watching a bunch of idiots get their heads ripped off for making stupid decisions will make me feel better about my stupid decision to have a casual sex weekend with my neighbour, right?"

The doorbell rang and Marmalade jumped off my lap with a loud hiss and spiked up fur. I winced and rubbed at my chest where her nails had dug in. I had no idea who was at my door at two thirty in the afternoon on Christmas Eve, but it could be a roving band of Christian evangelists for all I cared. I would invite them in to tell me all about their Lord and Saviour, if it meant a respite from my crushing loneliness.

I opened the front door, my mouth turning up in a stupid grin and happiness blossoming in my chest. "Hi!"

"Hi, Tess!" Oscar pushed his way past Sam and wrapped his arms around my leg. "Santa comes tonight!"

"I've heard." I leaned down and kissed his forehead. "Are you having a good day?"

"Yup." He kicked off his boots, a smile lighting up his face when he saw Marmalade. "Marmalade! Hi kitty."

He followed her into the living room as Sam took off his boots and hung his jacket on the hook. "Hi, Tess."

"Hi, Sam. How are you?"

"Good." He walked to the kitchen like he belonged here. I still had the stupid grin on my face, but I couldn't help it. I hadn't expected to see him until the twenty-seventh, and just having him in my house gave my growing depression a swift kick in its ass.

I followed him into the kitchen, blinking in surprise when he opened the pantry and took out one of the fabric shopping bags. He put the bag of taco chips in it and the unopened jar of salsa before moving to the fridge.

"Sam? What are you doing?"

"Packing up the nacho ingredients," he said.

"What?" I touched his arm. "Why are you taking my nacho ingredients?"

"Why didn't you tell me you were alone at Christmas?" he countered.

My face reddened. "Because it's embarrassing."

He frowned at me. "No, it isn't. You should have told me, Tess."

"I didn't want you to feel sorry for me."

"You're spending Christmas with us," he said.

I sighed. "See? This is why I didn't say anything. I don't need a pity invite, Sam."

"It isn't," he said. "The only reason I didn't ask you was because I stupidly assumed you would have plans. I want you to spend Christmas with us, Tess."

"It will give Oscar the wrong idea," I said.

"What? That we like spending Christmas with our friends?" He opened the fridge and added the ground beef, cheese, and sour cream to the bag. "Pack an overnight bag."

"What? Why?" I said.

"Because you're spending Christmas Day with us as well." He closed the fridge and smiled at me.

"Okay, but I can just come over in the morning," I said.

"No. You're not waking up alone on Christmas Day," he said.

"Sam, I can't stay the night. Oscar will -"

"Oscar?" Sam called.

Oscar walked into the kitchen, holding Marmalade. "What?"

"What do you think about Tess and Marmalade having a sleepover at our house tonight?"

"Yeah!" Oscar said. "We'll have nachos and hot chocolate, and Tess can help me put out the cookies for Santa."

Sam gave me an adorable *there you have it* look. "Run upstairs and pack your pajamas."

I hesitated and Oscar grinned at me. "Hurry up, Tess."

"Yeah, Tess. Hurry up," Sam said with a sexy little grin.

I gave in to what I truly wanted for Christmas. "Give me five minutes."

❧ ❦

"Oscar, those cookies are for Santa," Sam chided gently.

"I don't even know where you're putting that cookie," I said. "You ate a lot of nachos."

"They were good." Oscar set the plate of cookies on the small TV tray Sam had set up between the fireplace and the Christmas tree. "Daddy, do you have the carrots?"

Sam handed him the carrots and Oscar carefully arranged them on the TV tray. "Milk, Tess."

I gave him the glass of milk, watching with a smile on my face as he placed it next to the plate of cookies.

"What time do you think Santa will be here?" he said with careful indifference.

Sam laughed. "Too late for you to see him. Besides, you have to be in bed when he arrives or he'll be too shy to come down the chimney, remember?"

"Right." Oscar leaned against my legs. I smoothed his hair back from his face when he smiled up at me. "On Christmas Eve, Daddy lets me sleep in his bed with him even though I'm a big kid now. But he lets me 'cause it's a special day."

"That sounds like a lot of fun," I said.

"Actually, Oscar," Sam said. "I was thinking that maybe this Christmas, you could sleep in your bed."

"No!" Oscar's face drew down into a pout. "Daddy, no. You said I could sleep with you."

He stared up at me again. "Tess, tell Daddy he has to let me. I always sleep with him on Christmas Eve. We watch *Frosty the Snowman*, *Rudolph the Reindeer,* and *Elf.* Then Daddy reads to me until I fall asleep."

Tears were starting to gather in his eyes. I crouched and gave him a quick hug. "Of course, Daddy will do all those things. Don't cry, honey."

Oscar stared at Sam who nodded. "We will, buddy. I'm sorry. I didn't mean to upset you."

Oscar took my hand. "You can sleep in my bed tonight, Tess."

"Thanks, Oscar. That's very nice of you."

Sam muttered something under his breath that might have been a curse as Oscar said, "And you can sit in Daddy's bed and watch Frosty and Rudolph with us, but then you have to leave because it's my time with Daddy."

"Oscar," Sam said, "Tess is our guest for Christmas and that means she gets to do the same things we do."

"Well, I said she could watch Frosty and Rudolph with us," Oscar said.

"Oscar," Sam warned.

I kissed Oscar's forehead. "Thank you, Oscar. I would love to watch them with you. And then I promise to leave so you and Daddy can do your own thing. Okay?"

"Tess, you don't have to -"

"I don't mind," I said before Sam could finish. "Now, what time do we start the movie watching festivities?"

"Now," Oscar said. "But we gotta get in our pajamas first and Daddy has to make hot chocolate."

"You heard the kid," I said to Sam with a small grin. "Get making that hot chocolate."

Chapter Fourteen

Sam

I woke up at six to an empty bed. I sat up, scrubbing a hand through my hair before turning on the bedside lamp. I had to admit that while I'd enjoyed the night with Oscar, it hadn't exactly been the way I'd planned on spending Christmas Eve. My idea of making love to Tess in front of the fireplace with nothing but the glow of the fire and the Christmas tree lights on her soft skin, hadn't happened.

True to her word, Tess left my bed after we watched Frosty and Rudolph. Excited about Christmas and hopped up on sugar and a truly epic size portion of nachos, Oscar stayed awake through all of *Elf,* and I had to read three books before he finally nodded off around one.

I'd immediately crept to his room, only to find Tess curled up in Oscar's bed and sound asleep. She was flanked by Marmalade and Jack and the two cats didn't move when I leaned over and kissed Tess's forehead.

She didn't wake, and I'd left her sleeping and went downstairs. I'd put the presents from Santa under the tree and filled Oscar's stocking. I ate a couple of the cookies, drank the milk, and broke off half the carrots before returning to my own bed. I wanted Tess, wanted to sink myself into her soft, warm body, but she'd been sleeping so deeply I hated to wake her. Besides, after the sleepless night before, I was tired myself. If I'd wanted to be in any shape to handle Oscar's excitement on Christmas, I'd needed rest.

I slid out of bed and used the bathroom before leaving the bedroom. I expected Oscar to wake up early, but I also expected him to wake me up. I cocked my head, listening carefully. There were no noises coming from downstairs. In fact, the house was completely silent.

I walked to Oscar's bedroom, sticking my head inside the room. My breath caught in my throat. At some point, Oscar had left my bed and joined Tess in his. The two of them were curled up in the bed together, Oscar's arms flung around Tess and her arm curled protectively around him.

My heart beating hard, I stared at them for a long time as both Jack and Marmalade jumped off the bed and rubbed up against my legs. I moved to the bed and turned the beside lamp on. I sat down on the side of the bed behind Tess's legs, resting my hand on her hip and rubbing lightly. She didn't stir but Oscar made a snorting noise before his eyes blinked open.

He starred blurrily at me before staring at Tess, a small smile crossing his face. "Tess is pretty, huh?"

"She is," I said.

"I love her," he said before sitting up.

My chest tightened and it was suddenly hard to swallow. "I love her too, buddy."

"I know," he said. "Are you going to ask her to be your girlfriend?"

"I am," I said. "What do you think about that?"

Tess opened her eyes, blinking at us like a sleepy owl, before saying, "What time is it?"

"Early," I said.

Oscar's eyes widened. "Daddy! It's Christmas! Did Santa come? Did he?"

"I don't know," I said. "Maybe you should go downstairs and find out."

He slid out of the bed, nearly dancing with excitement. "C'mon, Jack!" he shouted. "Let's see what Santa brought us!"

He raced out of his bedroom. Tess smiled and sat up, the smile widening when she heard him thunder down the stairs and then his whoop of happiness.

"How did you sleep?" I rubbed her hip again as she stretched.

"Surprisingly well, considering how small Oscar's bed is," she said. "He came into his room around three and climbed into the bed. I wasn't sure if I should return him to your bed, but he insisted he wanted to sleep with me."

"That's fine. Thank you for last night," I said. "For being so understanding about Oscar and his

Christmas ritual."

"Of course." She cupped my face, her thumb rubbing across my cheekbone. "Sam, I want Oscar to be happy. You know that, right?"

"I know," I said. "Tess, I have something I need to say. I don't want just -"

"Daddy!" Oscar was at the bottom of the stairs, shrieking louder than a marine drill instructor. "Santa was here! He was here! Come downstairs!"

Tess laughed and slid out of the bed. "I think he wants you to come downstairs."

"Yeah," I said.

She was gathering her hair into a bun and I stood. "Tess, I -"

"DADDY!"

"You'd better go before he wakes the whole neighbourhood," she said with another laugh. "I'm just going to use the washroom and then I'll join you."

"All right," I said. I stared at her for a little longer, memorizing the sweetness of her face in the pale light of the lamp.

She gave me a curious look. "What?"

"Nothing. I'll see you downstairs."

Tess

"Oscar, what do you say to Tess?" Sam finished tugging the shirt over Oscar's head.

"Thank you, Tess. I love my new Wonder Woman shirt." Oscar snatched up the plush Spiderman toy I'd also gotten him and held it up in

153

the air. "No, Jack. You have your own toys. This is mine."

He searched through the wrapping paper thrown on the floor and found the cat wand toy. Within seconds, he was twirling it and giggling wildly as Jack and Marmalade chased after the toy. He'd finished opening his gifts and while he'd gotten some really cool toys, I was ridiculously pleased that my gifts had gone over so well with him.

"Thank you for my gift," Sam said. He held the bobblehead figurines of Danny and Sandy from *Grease* to his chest and tilted his head. "I will treasure them always."

I laughed and poked him in the stomach. "I told you it wasn't anything big."

He grinned, and I nearly fell off the couch when he leaned over and kissed me on the mouth. "Seriously, I love them. It's the perfect gift."

I touched my mouth, glancing over at Oscar who was still playing with the cats. "Um, I guess we should get the turkey in the oven, right?"

It was a ridiculous thing to say after being kissed, but I wasn't sure what to say or do.

"In a minute," Sam said. "You haven't opened our present yet."

"You got me a present?" I said.

"We did. Oscar, grab Tess's present from under the tree, would you?"

Oscar snagged the last box wrapped in bright red paper from under the tree. He brought it over and climbed into Sam's lap, handing me the present. "Open it, Tess."

Smiling at him, I tore off the paper before

opening up the box. I stared at the stethoscope nestled in tissue paper. Tears pricking at my eyes, I scooped it out of the box. "Sam, I… I love it."

"It's for when you start animal school," Oscar said. He took the stethoscope from me and hooked it around his neck. "I wanted to get you a Wonder Woman comic book, but Daddy said you would like this better. Do you, Tess?"

"I love it," I said. "Thank you, Oscar."

"You're welcome."

"Thank you, Sam."

"You're welcome, Tess." The look in Sam's eyes made me feel a bit breathless and a whole lot confused.

"Sam, what -"

"I have something I wanted to ask you," he said. "I talked to Oscar and -"

"He thinks you're pretty and wants you to be his girlfriend," Oscar said.

Sam actually blushed. "Way to ruin the moment, Oscar."

"What moment?" Oscar looked from his dad to me and then back to his dad. "You said you were going to ask her to be your girlfriend. Remember?"

"I remember," Sam said.

Oscar turned to me. "Tess, are you gonna… why are you crying?"

"Because I'm happy." I swiped at the tears on my face.

"People don't cry when they're happy." Oscar made a face before sliding off Sam's lap and putting my stethoscope on the coffee table. "I'm gonna get some cereal."

I stared wide-eyed at Sam as Oscar left the living room. He smiled and pulled me into his lap before pressing a kiss against my mouth. "Well, Ms. Walker, what do you say? Will you be my girlfriend?"

"Why have you changed your mind?" I said.

"Because you're amazing and kind, and you're incredible with Oscar and he loves you. He told me that this morning."

"I love him too," I said.

"I know." Sam rested his forehead against mine. "You love my kid, and you want him to be happy. You're warm and generous, and sweet and so damn sexy, I can't stand it. I want more than just a casual sex arrangement, Tess. I want you in my life and in my kid's life. What do you say? Will you give dating me a chance?"

"Yes, absolutely one hundred percent yes," I said.

He kissed me hard on the mouth, his tongue sliding between my lips to taste and tease.

"You should know," he said when we came up for air, "that I'm pretty sure I'm falling in love with you, Ms. Walker."

"What a coincidence, Mr. Black," I said. "I'm pretty sure I'm falling in love with you too."

His smile was sexy and sweet at the same time. "Merry Christmas, Tess."

"Merry Christmas, Sam."

Epilogue

One year later

Tess

"Tess! Tess, we're home!" Oscar's voice echoed through the house.

"In the kitchen," I called.

He burst into the kitchen in a flurry of cold air and excitement. I smiled at him. "Hey, kiddo, how was school?"

"Good. Mrs. Preston let us sit and read our books for the last hour because it was the last day of school."

Sam walked into the kitchen, his cheeks red from the cold and his suit covered in a heavy dusting of snow. "It's really coming down out there. I'm glad we're not going anywhere for Christmas."

He kissed me, his hand sliding around to squeeze my ass as Oscar grabbed some juice from

157

the fridge. "How was your day, honey?"

"Good. Like Oscar, our teacher let us sit and read for the last hour of class too. Only I was reading all about the anatomy of a mammal," I said with a grin.

"Nice. Did you get a chance to stop at the grocery store on the way home for the nacho stuff or are we braving the Christmas Eve last minute shoppers tomorrow?"

"We are good to go," I said. "The amount of groceries we have in this house, we could spend the next two weeks of winter break entirely at home if we wanted."

"Noah's mom is picking me up on Boxing Day to go to the cabin," Oscar said a bit anxiously. "Did you forget, Tess?"

"No," I said. "I know you're going to the cabin with Noah and his family."

"Okay, just checking," Oscar said. "I'm gonna be gone for five whole days. You and Daddy are gonna be bored without me."

"Oh, I think we can find ways to kill the boredom," Sam said. His hand squeezed my butt again and his smile held a sexy promise.

"Hey, did you remember to text Alton that we're a yes for the New Year's Eve party?" I said.

"Yep," he said. "You sure you want to hang out with a bunch of theatre nerds on New Year's Eve?"

"I wouldn't miss it," I said. "If I'm really lucky, you guys will do a spontaneous re-enactment of that part in the play where you all take off your pants and dance around in your underwear."

"I don't remember that part and I've seen

Daddy's play three times," Oscar said. "Twice with you and once with Uncle Elliot."

"Wait," I said, "that was the Fourth of July party where you all dropped your pants and danced around in your underwear."

Oscar shook his head. "Grown-ups are weird."

Sam and I laughed, and he winked at me before heading toward the stairs. "C'mon, buddy. Let's change out of our clothes before we help Tess cook dinner."

"Sure." Oscar gave his dad a furtive and secretive look. "Are we gonna do the thing before dinner, Daddy?"

"What thing?" I said.

"Nothing!" Oscar's eyes widened and he stared at Sam. "Nothing, right, Daddy?"

"C'mon, bud." Sam held out his hand. Giving me another weird look, Oscar grabbed Sam's hand and followed him up the stairs.

I turned back to the potatoes and picked up another one to peel. Four months after we'd started dating, Sam had asked me to move in with him and Oscar. I couldn't say yes fast enough. I smiled and stared out the window at the snow falling. The last year had been the happiest of my life. I loved being in school to be a vet tech and I loved Sam and Oscar. My life couldn't be more perfect.

I finished peeling the potatoes and rinsed them before filling the pot with water and setting it on the stove. I'd already put the chicken in the oven, but I'd get Oscar to help me chop up the vegetables for the salad. He loved helping out in the kitchen and despite the fact that he was still in ballet classes and loving it, I had a feeling that he was headed for a career in the culinary arts.

I hoped so, I mused. It would be handy to have a chef in the family, especially during holidays and -

"Tess?" Oscar's voice was unusually shy. I turned around and my jaw dropped. Sam was on one knee and Oscar was standing next to him, holding out an open ring box. I stared at the ring nestled inside of it as Sam cleared his throat.

"Tess, I love you. You make me so happy and - "

"And me," Oscar said. "You make me happy too."

"You make *us* happy," Sam said with a small smile. "We can't imagine our lives without you. I want to spend the rest of my life with you. Will you marry me?"

Already starting to cry, I nodded wildly. "Yes. Yes, Sam, I'll marry you."

Sam gave Oscar a boyish look of delight. I cracked up laughing when he held up his hand and Oscar high-fived him. Sam took the ring out of the box and slid it onto my finger before standing.

I threw my arms around him and kissed him hard on the mouth before admiring the ring. "Oh my God, it's so beautiful, Sam."

"Oscar helped me pick it out."

I crouched and hugged Oscar. "Thank you, honey."

"I love you, Tess," he said.

"I love you too, honey." I hugged him again, smiling at him when he leaned back to stare at me.

"I'm so happy to be a part of your family, Oscar."

"I was thinking that maybe I'd call you mom," he said. "If that's okay with you?"

Sam inhaled sharply above me. I glanced up at him and he nodded before wiping at the tears that were starting to slide down his cheeks.

I didn't bother to wipe away my tears as I smiled at Oscar. "Honey, nothing would make me happier than you calling me mom."

He grinned at me and I kissed his forehead before standing.

"Cool," he said. "I'm gonna find Jack and Marmalade and tell them you're getting married."

He skipped out of the kitchen and I stared at Sam. "Are you sure you're okay with him calling me mom?"

Sam nodded, his voice hoarse when he said, "Yes. I really am."

I wiped away the lingering traces of tears on his face before kissing him. "I love you, Sam. I can't wait to be your wife."

"I love you too, Tess. Always."

END

Please enjoy an excerpt of Elizabeth Kelly's novel
"SORDID GAMES"

SORDID GAMES
Copyright ©2018 Elizabeth Kelly

Daisy

I was nervous. I didn't want to be, I wanted to look sexy and confident, but the way my hand shook when I tried to insert the card key into the lock, didn't exactly scream confidence. Wes's big hand covered mine and he helped me insert the card into the slot. The red light turned green and I opened the door before stepping out of the cold air and into the room. As I fumbled for the light, I had a sudden dismaying thought. What if Frannie was here? What if she had finished with Owen and was sleeping in the second double bed?

She won't be. She's spending the night with Owen and you know that, you goober. Relax for God's sake. Just because you're about to get naked and have sex with the perfect man doesn't mean you have to act like a complete idiot.

I took a deep breath. My inner voice was right. Besides, maybe Wes was good looking and funny and smart. Maybe the little dimple that showed up in his right cheek every time he smiled at me made me nearly drip with anticipation. But he wasn't perfect. No one was.

He looks perfect.

He looked perfect, but he wasn't. He probably had, I don't know, a small dick. I seized on that thought almost desperately. Yes, he probably had a small dick and was terrible in bed. He probably sucked at sex and it would be awkward and weird, and my first one-night stand would be a complete bust.

"Daisy?"

I realized we were still standing in the doorway in the dark and I hurriedly found the switch and flipped it on. Both double beds were empty, and I took a deep breath before turning to smile at Wes. "Sorry."

He studied me carefully. The door was still open, and coldness was creeping into the room.

"Are you going to shut the door?" I crossed my arms nervously over my torso.

"If you've changed your mind, I can leave."

I blinked at him. "I – I haven't changed my mind. Have you?"

"No, but you look nervous."

"I am nervous," I admitted.

"Don't be." He shut the door and locked it before taking off his boots. I kicked mine off and held my hand out for his jacket. He handed it to me, and I tossed them onto Frannie's bed.

"Easy for you to say," I said. "You're really handsome and have the perfect body so…"

I studied the cheap carpet under my feet. What was wrong with me? I usually had more self-confidence than this in bed. Of course, I hadn't been with anyone but Richard in the last two and a half years. Richard was used to the scar on my tummy from my appendectomy, my weirdly long toes, and the –

I suddenly froze and gave Wes a look of panic. "Oh shit."

"What?" He was reaching for me and he stopped immediately. "What's wrong?"

"I haven't shaved."

He laughed. "I haven't shaved either."

"You don't understand," I said. "I haven't shaved in *weeks*. We're at Sasquatch levels of hair."

"I really don't care if your legs aren't shaved, Daisy. I swear." Wes reached down and adjusted the obvious bulge at the front of his jeans. "Let me show you how much I don't care."

"It's, uh, not just my legs." I glanced at my crotch. "I haven't exactly kept up with my, uh, waxing routine since I've been single."

Wes followed my gaze to my crotch, and I turned bright red. "You know what? Let's turn the lights off."

"Are you kidding me?" Wes said teasingly. "You can't tell me something like that and then expect me not to look."

"No way," I said. "I want the lights off and both of us under the covers."

Wes grabbed my hand before I could shut off the lights. "Sorry, darlin', but that's not happening." He pulled me into his arms and kissed me until I was clinging to him and panting. He kissed his way to my ear and sucked on my earlobe. "I want to see every inch of your tight little body tonight."

ॐ ॐ

About the Author

Elizabeth Kelly was born and raised in Ontario, Canada. She moved west as a teenager and now lives in Alberta with her husband and a menagerie of pets. She firmly believes that a human can survive solely on sushi and coffee, and only her husband's mad cooking skills stops her from proving that theory.

If you would like more information about Elizabeth, please visit her at:

www.elizabethkelly.ca

Books by Elizabeth Kelly

Individual Books

The Necessary Engagement
Amelia's Touch
The Rancher's Daughter
Healing Gabriel
The Contract
A Home for Lily
Saving Charlotte
The Christmas Wife
Shameless
The Fairy Tales Collection
Broken
An Unlikely Seduction
Sordid Games
The Christmas Rescue
The Christmas Nanny

Tempted Series

Tempted
Twice Tempted
Tempted 3
Breathless

Red Moon Series

Red Moon
Red Moon Rising
Dark Moon
Alpha Moon
Pale Moon

The Recruit Series

The Recruit (Book One)
The Recruit (Book Two)
The Recruit (Book Three)
The Recruit (Book Four)
The Recruit (Book Five)
The Recruit (Book Six)

The Shifters Series

Willow and the Wolf (Book One)
Ava and the Bear (Book Two)
Katarina and the Bird (Book Three)
Porter's Mate (Book Four)
Bria and the Tiger (Book Five)
Rosalie Undone (Book Six)
The Dragon's Mate (Book Seven)

The Draax Series

Reign (Book One)
Rule (Book Two)
Rebel (Book Three)

Harmony Falls Series

Sweet Harmony (Book One)
Perfect Harmony (Book Two)
Forbidden Harmony (Book Three)
Redeeming Harmony (Book Four)

Made in the USA
Middletown, DE
16 December 2020

28470897R00096